PART ONE

OMISSION

FATE'S BITE SERIES

SHE'S THE PRIZE AT THE END OF
MY BATTLES. WHO I WILL KILL FOR

ELENA M. REYES

SUMMARY

I'M A KING.
A PROTECTOR.
IRREVOCABLY HERS.

Since birth, I've been surrounded by the enemy—those who wish to destroy the essence of my kind's existence, but have failed to at every turn. For greed. Because of ignorance. And while I've vowed to drive a sword through their hearts and display their heads outside our royal grounds, I will never harm *her*.

A divine rule etched into the very magic that flows through my veins, even if she's the daughter of the man who murdered my parents. Even if her people aren't to be trusted.

Yet there's one truth I could never deny:

This lovely little doll is mine.

One look into her warm violet eyes, and my world stops. She's where I begin and now end—the prize at the end of my battles. Who I will kill for.

"Mate."

OMISSION
Part One (Fate's Bite #5)
was written by Elena M. Reyes
Copyright 2023 ©Elena M. Reyes

Cover Design: T.E. Black Designs
Editor: Marti Lynch

Publication Date: December 11th, 2023
Genre: FICTION/Dark Romance/Erotic Suspense/Paranormal
Copyright © 2023 Elena M. Reyes

ACKNOWLEDGMENTS

This one is for you, my readers.
Thank you for all the love and support while your girl has been struggling with her health. I appreciate every message, email, and kind words you've sent me.
They have gotten me through really rough days and made me smile.
I truly love you with all my heart.

Elena XoXo

ELECTRICITY SPARKS WHERE I
TOUCH HER, MY COCK
THROBBING AS I GET THE FIRST
FEEL OF HER DELICIOUS CURVES
PINNED BENEATH ME.

PART ONE

OMISSION

FATE'S BITE SERIES

ELENA M. REYES

PART ONE

OMISSION

FATE'S BITE SERIES

playlist

BLACK HOLE SUN BY SOUNDGARDEN
INTO THE DARKNESS BY THE PHANTOMS
SHADOW OF THE DAY BY LINKIN PARK
WELCOME TO THE FIRE BY WILLYECHO
TURNING PAGE BY SLEEPING AT LAST
I COULD FALL IN LOVE BY SELENA
CALLING YOU BY BLUE OCTOBER
AUTEUR BY SAINT MESA
I WANNA BE YOURS BY ARCTIC MONKEYS
BETWEEN RAINDROPS BY LIFEHOUSE &
NATASHA BEDINGFIELD

PART ONE

playlist

EVERYTHING BY LIFEHOUSE
MI VERDAD BY MANA & SHAKIRA
FAVORITO BY CAMILO
PHOTOGRAPH BY ED SHEERAN
BUILT BY NATIONS BY GRETA VAN FLEET
ANIMAL I HAVE BECOME BY THREE DAYS GRACE
NIGHT VIVE BY SKYFALL BEATS
HIGHWAY TUNE BY GRETA VAN FLEET
OCEAN BY KAROL G
YOUNG AND BEAUTIFUL BY LANA DEL REY

TRIGGER WARNINGS:

This book contains dark elements that some readers might find triggering. This man is brutal and unapologetic, please read at your own discretion.

Contains:

Explicit Violence (GORE)
Death & Torture
Biting/Mating Mark
Abusive family
Misogynistic Male Family Members
Possessive Anti-Hero
Threatening of FMC
Abuse of FMC by Villain (Not Sexual)
Some Blood Play/Licking During Sex (Bite or Cut)
Fated Mates
Drugging/Poisoning of FMC by Villain

Loving you will never be easy,
but it'll be my greatest honor
to call you mine.
My wife.
My female.
My precious one.
Many have bled so that one day,
I'd wake with you in my arms. So
that I'd know what it's like to
love someone so fully—so
irrevocably—that the true
meaning of unselfish sacrifice is
forever tattooed in my DNA.
I will always love you, Anaya.
You are forever my gift.
Your Mate.
Your Warlock.
Your King.

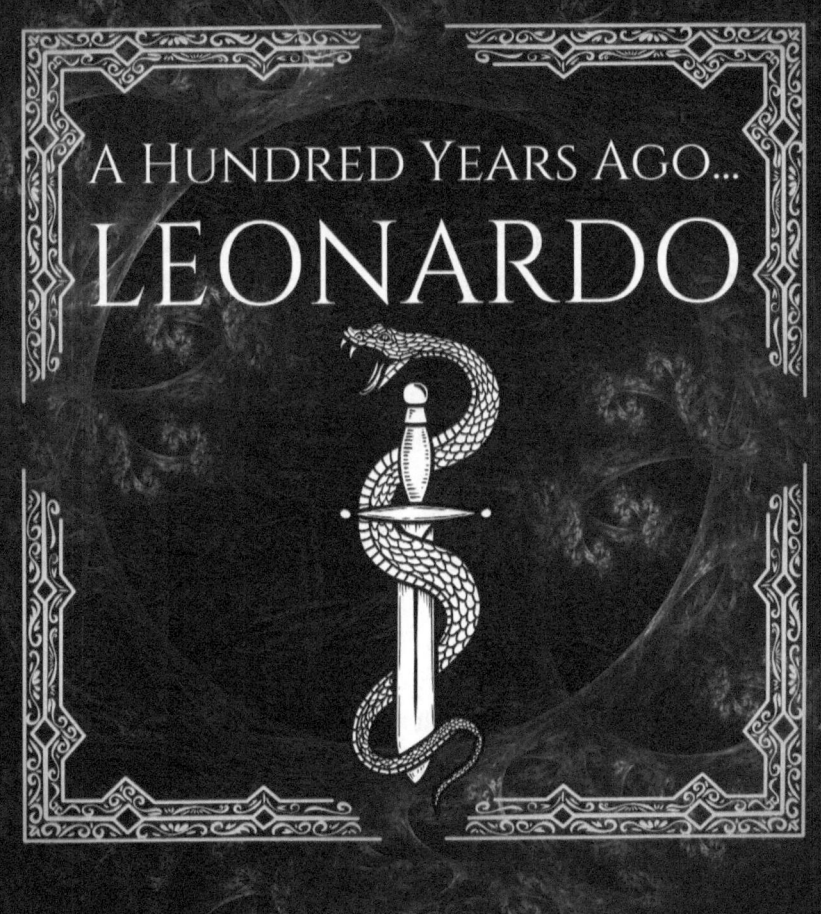

A HUNDRED YEARS AGO...
LEONARDO

"Please don't do this. There has to be another way." My words are low, a whisper drowned out by the sound of our enemies battering the manor's front door. It's loud and haunting. The endless pounding of a large object reverberates as it slams against the wooden structure—vibrates through every object within these walls—and yet, I know they heard every word.

It's there in the trembling of my father's hand on my right shoulder and the harsh bob of his throat. In the tightness around his eyes as the king of all Wiccans fights back his emotions. How our mother cries; each tear follows the track left behind by the previous drops while her entire body shakes.

Both are in pain but refuse to fight.

Both listen to our pleas and arguments, yet nothing has changed.

Instead, they try to pretend everything will be okay—that we'll survive this—but the truth can't be hidden behind forced smiles when so much pain permeates through our bond. When I can see just how much this is destroying them. Hurts more than the betrayal from those they once considered family.

Minutes are all we have left now. Seconds. And each tick of the clock is a stark reminder of everything we'll lose once those fighting to enter our home do so.

Because they will. A fate foretold can never be changed, and while the path traveled might deviate in certain situations, the destination is always the same. Each cause has an effect. For every action, there's an equal consequence you can't outrun for long:

The blood of many witches will bathe these grounds tonight. And if they are my kin, I'll one day kill those responsible in their honor.

"Leo, everything will be as it should. Trust in yourself and—"

"Why are you just giving up? You can stop this." My tone is harsh and bitter as my chest races while sharp, emotional lashes strike my body. And yet, I pay it no mind as my eyes ping from my family to the door protecting this room and then back again. There isn't a second to spare in convincing them—to try to make our parents understand—when only a few walls are separating the enemy from us, and they'll be inside soon enough. "Maybe there's something we missed or overlooked? We need more time to figure this out."

"No."

"Father, why can't we use a portal to Uncle Roberto's house?" Although he tries to hide it, I still catch the slight tensing of his jaw at my words. How a low growl slips at his brother's name. "We need to buy ourselves time."

"Stop this. We won't."

"What do you mean? Why aren't you—"

"Calm yourself, young king." It's a stern reproach, his voice leaving no room for argument, and I nod while biting back my anger. Instead, I take a moment to refocus my attention—to get control over my limbs that never cease their trembling as I fight against every emotion threatening to consume me.

Two of their children are drowning in this purgatory while the third one sleeps, oblivious and hidden within a false sense of safety, and he knows this. Moreover, I'm full of ire. So much disappointment.

At them, for leaving us behind when my father—the most powerful Wiccan among us—can end this before it even begins. At myself, as the future king and being unable to save them. Magic vibrates beneath my skin, tugging at my essence, but it doesn't show itself yet. Because at only thirteen summers, I've yet to start my training. Would've begun after the next solstice, but that's unimportant now.

"You will go with Isa and Gabby, Leo. They will protect and guide you."

"It should be you." The words are harsh, bathed in my hurt, and I wish I could take them back immediately. Not because they're not true, but because this can't be the last words I say to him.

Gods, don't abandon us. Aid us.

"I know." Remorse. So much anguish in those two simple words as his eyes glisten, and yet the tears don't fall. Instead, the metaphysical flow of his power wraps around me in a warm embrace, and the sorrow-filled whimper that comes from Isabella tells me he's reached out to her, too. It's something he's done for as long as I can remember, a way to calm and soothe his children when faced with the unknown: a spell or unfamiliar terrain—the news that soon, we'll never see each other again in this realm. "And I'm so sorry, son. I wish there was another way, but I'll always forfeit my life so that you three thrive. It's my honor as your father to do so."

Another loud bang rings throughout, and a thunderous crack

follows. It pulls a frightened noise from my sister and mother, both hugging now while the latter gives her daughter the comfort she needs, but then Isa pulls away and wipes at her face harshly. There's a set determination in her expression that mixes with a feeling of helplessness that mimics my own.

She extends a shaking hand toward our king. "Father, please. It's not too late."

"You can't outrun fate, Isabella. You both know this." And we do, but that doesn't make this any easier. If anything, I feel as though a noose is tightening around my neck—my chest aches—but I maintain enough composure to not lash out. It's the only thing I have control over; a lesson given to all royal children from birth. "Daughter, you've seen what I've seen and the end for those involved. Never falter, sweet child. You three are our future, and many will depend on you."

"But we need you."

How are we supposed to just accept this?

"My babies, please go." Mom looks at me and then Isabella while the sounds coming from our front door grow louder. Each strike is harder than the last, and the walls shake—it feels as though the very ground we stand upon already mourns its leaders. Then, there's the clash of fighting and the screams of those caught between them and us. Our loyal guards refuse to back down. Our blood soaking the ground is what these traitors want. "Get Leo out of here. You three are our future, Isa. Save our people."

"Gabriella should be here." At my muttered words, Dad grips my shoulders and turns me to fully face him. He bends low enough that he's able to lay his forehead over mine, and for a minute neither of us speaks while I give in to the mental block he's now providing. Father mouths the word *silentium* and all noise around us becomes a low thrum in the background. All movement freezes, and my breathing becomes easier.

"Better?"

"Yes."

"Good. Now I need you to listen—"

"Please, Dad. I'm begging you." He shakes his head in response, and that's when I finally let my tears fall, a sight that breaks him. His fall, too. They match mine, and I hate it. All of this. My father is powerful, more so than any other of our kind on these lands, but he refuses to stop this witch hunt. "Why? We need you."

"And one day these lands will thrive with you as their king. My time as ruler ends here; they need you, Leonardo, not me." He's said this before. Many times, in fact, but right now I don't want to hear it. Not when the scent of death surrounding his tall frame intensifies and clings, permeating every inch of this room. Just like it does to our mother. "And as my heir, you know this to be true. Our selfish desires can never rise above the needs of our people. We guide, nurture, and protect."

"Will nothing change your mind?"

"No."

A sharp breath chokes out of me, and it feels as though some-one's punched me in the gut, but I can't move or respond. I'm left to stand still and hunch further into myself, a hand coming up to rub at the area where my heart bleeds inside my chest while those around me continue to talk. I can make out Isa trying one last time. I can sense our family moving in a little closer, but it isn't until the thick wood of our home's front door splinters that I react.

Everything slams into my processors faster than I can comprehend.

There's the cracking of the entrance and how the remnants slam into the wall or floor.

The sound of shouting infiltrating every square inch of our home; the cries of victory from the very same men who've come to kill us. They curse our very existence while the blood that runs through their veins is Wiccan.

Instantly, I'm filled with anger. So much so that my hands shake and then begin to disappear, something my father stops by placing his large one over mine. He shakes his head at me; in his eyes, there's pride and love, but also worry. No one knows what my powers will be, but this is a sign he'd rather stay hidden.

Control it, my son. Not here. My response to his mental message is a minute nod of the head and he exhales roughly, swallowing hard. "I'm proud of you. Know that I will always be with you."

My head's shaking before he's done speaking. My bottom lip trembles because, at thirteen summers, I'm seeing the world for what it is: cruel and fueled by greed. "I don't want to say goodbye."

"Then don't. This is more of an *I'll see you later.*"

"Okay." A broken whisper.

"Good. Now, I need you to listen to me, and don't interrupt." Those inside the home are tearing it apart, the shattering of glass and knocking over of furniture closer now, but they can't get through yet. The heavy and protected door to this room will keep them out for a little longer. Not much. Never enough. "Do you remember the book I gave you a few nights ago? The one with the thick binding on ancient translations?" My response is a nod; I remember it—hid it inside my room under a loose floorboard. I know it's important. "Someday she'll need that book to save Gabby. Remind her when it happens."

"I will," I say through the boulder-like lumps in my throat. "Promise."

"Thank you, my king." For a second he bows his head in my direction, a show of respect from one ruler to another, even if it shouldn't be my time yet. "Keep it safe because you'll need it more than once."

"Dad, I—"

"And two, as you grow up, I want you to remember the lessons I've taught you. Never forget that volatile emotions are uncontrollable and will kill you from within. That you must always be fair and just, and lead our people without prejudice over what's happened here today. Don't dishonor my memory by placing the blame on an innocent's head because of mere association. Not everything is as it seems."

"What did you see? Who are you talking about?"

"Love is the most powerful thing in the world, Leo. No matter the species or your beliefs, we are all worthy of unconditional love, son. So when you find her, cherish your mate. Honor her and your bond, even if at times, this brings you pain."

CHAPTER 1
LEONARDO

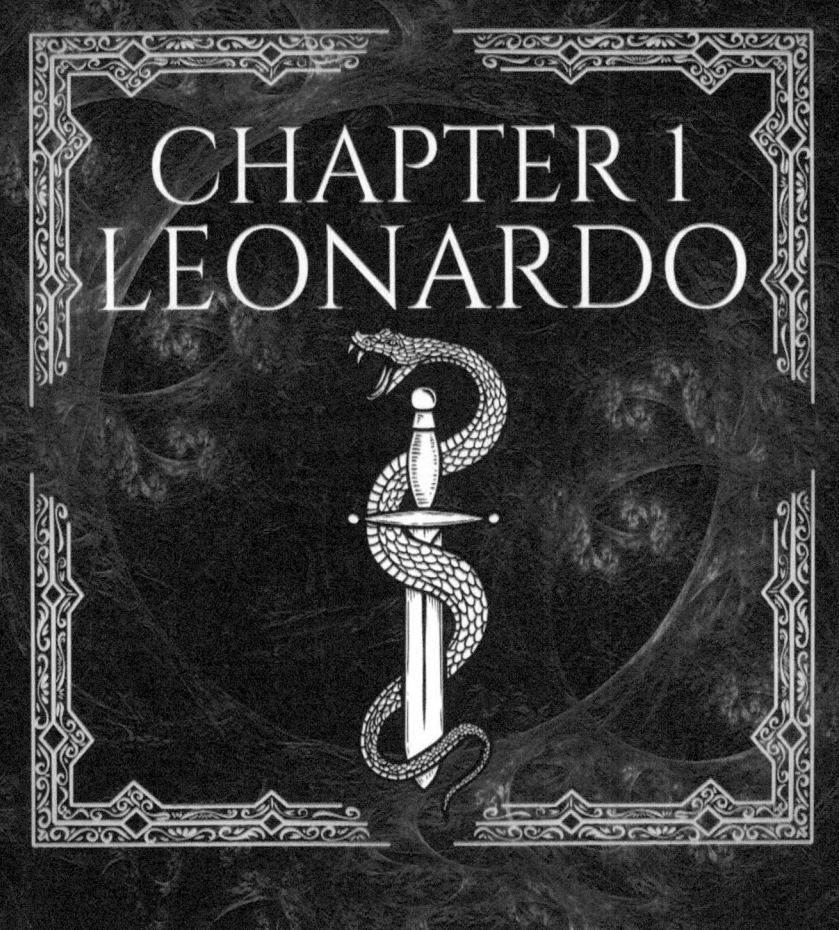

I 'm aware of *her* presence the very second she steps a single foot inside the room.

Each footfall is light; the soft clack of high-heeled shoes reverberates throughout the space even as chaos erupts all around me. There are shouts and threats. That decaying scent of flesh fills every square inch as death looms closer—it clings to those of fae blood—and I lick my lips as I get the first taste of revenge.

Promise made. Promise kept.

Emotions I share with my siblings. Our familial bonds vibrate; they're vacillating between ecstasy and the pang of memories that

9

will forever mark our lives, but then that too becomes a distant buzz as my attention shifts.

Everything stops because of this wonderous slip of a girl.

Because I know who this female is. What she represents as old and new wounds tear open and I'm slammed by the desires I've kept hidden for much longer than she's been alive.

For a new beginning. For the gift promised by the gods.

Can I accept this fae female? The daughter of my enemy?

I'm frozen in place for a minute as I take her in while no one notices the change in my demeanor. She's unsure, afraid—needs someone to save her from the demonic claws that keep her here—while I'm fighting to control my powers as the molecular structure of everything around me bends.

Everything, but her. She's the center of my focus.

And as I watch her, a voice I haven't heard in a long time infiltrates my thoughts. It's a welcomed intrusion, as is the feel of a warm hand on my shoulder. Even while cloaked in invisibility, the touch cuts through my magic.

I haven't felt my father's presence this strong in a long time—years—and never like this. Not even the ceremony held with my sisters a few weeks back created this strong of a connection, and the fact he's reciting the same words spoken to me before his death isn't lost on me either.

This is what he meant then.

He saw her. This moment.

Love is the most powerful thing in the world, Leo. No matter the species or your beliefs, we are all worthy of unconditional love, son. So when you find her, cherish your mate. Honor her and your bond, even if at times it brings you pain.

"Fuck." It slips from me, almost giving away my location, but no one hears. Not my family or the fae bastards still alive and currently protecting their king. There aren't many left, but they swim in the nauseating perfume; it clings to their skin, and it's not their natural fragrance.

Moreover, I've smelled this before. I would recognize the stench anywhere.

These people will die.

Thanatos is close; I can't see him, but I sense him. Someone else, too.

The volatile powers are stronger than any one of us, combined or alone, and I can't help but take a protective step toward my mate while Gabriella's aura darkens and the essence of life sways in her direction. While Isabella strikes, the sharp shards of glass rise high above the enemy's head and hold still.

Each one marks a fae.

Everyone but her. My female.

Then, there are the vibrations fluttering all around me as her soul calls out to mine. It's a shock to the system, this need that grows with each sweet breath that leaves her body and the way she leans my way. An unconscious move, almost undetectable, but I'm attuned to her every move.

To her.

Our bond tugs at the very core of me; a connection that finds its home inside my chest while simultaneously caressing my thickening cock in one smooth stroke, and more so when that first tendril of her scent infiltrates my senses. Drops of pre-come slip from my engorged head and roll down my shaft slowly, a feather-like touch, and I grit my teeth while my nostrils flare.

While my hands clench and unclench, my powers vibrate beneath my skin. I'm being burned alive, the abilities I possess keeping me hidden from all but her. She hasn't looked up yet, but her curves move in my direction, tipping just enough that one of the guards shifts his attention toward me. Not that he finds anything; I'm invisible, yet she senses me.

It's there in the tiny flare of her nostrils.

The goosebumps on her skin.

And I find myself following her lead and breathing deep, biting down on my lower lip to hide the groan that fights to break free. Rich and tempting; this tiny, curvaceous blonde female with the scent of strawberries and decadent cream reminds me of my favorite dessert. She smells like home and memories never forgotten and the warmth that's been missing from my life since the night of our parent's murder.

It's completion.

It's peace.

I need her.

My mouth waters as my cellular structure contracts—I can't control the reaction—and I glitch just long enough for King Larue and his piece of merda guards to take notice. I'm no longer concealed, and immediately their weapons are pointing in my direction as multiple rounds unload seconds after I've moved. Casings ping off the ground and *her* heartbeat begins to race, a beautiful cadence intertwining—dancing with the light blue aura she's emitting.

No one sees it. No one feels it.

Yet it's searching and stretching, flowing out from her petite form until she finds me beside an angry Xadiel, and I watch her exhale roughly. There's clear confusion on her face. None of this makes sense to her, but to me, her relief is palpable and bone-deep.

"Are you okay?" my brother-in-law says from beside me, half-shifted and breathing hard, his black-tipped talons dripping with the blood of his earlier kill. Then again, he isn't the only one with an overwhelming desire for vengeance—to finally put down the fae king and his followers as punishment for every crime committed against humanity and *others.* "What shook you? I felt it from here."

"I'm fine." Not that he sees me, but I make it so my voice is low enough to not be detected by the others in the room. My sisters hear me, though. In any other situation, it would be comical how their heads simultaneously tilt in my direction while each holds their ground. Not so much as a moment of reprieve is given to my mate's kin.

Yet as Larue orders Isabella to return to his side, I'm slammed into another memory. I'm here, but not—dragged back to my familial lands and the day the opal dagger in my right hand was given to me a century ago. Reliving the first time its sharp blade made contact with my open palm...

"Who's that?" I ask Isabella, voice low while watching the stranger closely. Not because I'm wary of him, but because there's this same sense of familiarity—bond—that I have with my sisters. Why?

"My kind of mate," Isa whispers back while her lips twitch. It's small and at the corner, but I catch it and I think he does too. There's also the way they angle their bodies toward each other, an unconscious mirroring that I think neither are aware of. The signs of being mates are there, just like Mom and Dad were, but something lingers.

Something she's hiding.

"For real?" I'm eyeing him from head to toe now while Isa watches me. Always overprotective and worried, but I keep that to myself. Her mate is a werewolf. An alpha, at that. "He's huge."

"You'll grow into the role, too, young king," he interjects, but I don't respond because what's now in his hand has my sole attention. It's wrapped in silk and the size gives away what it is, but that's not why I'm quick to grab and then unwrap it. The moment it's in my palm, the noise level around me dims a bit; not like Father was able to do, but the reprieve is a blessing.

The dagger is smooth and shiny with an opal-stoned hilt that vibrates in my hand. The movement is barely noticeable to the eye, but in my palm, it sinks into the flesh and merges as if we are one. Meant to be mine.

"This is so cool. Thank you, almost-mate-of-Isabella." I hear myself say this, but my eyes can't pull themselves away from the glinting blade and the words carved into the metal. An unknown language to me, but I see the scripture clear as day. Then, there's this low hum that merges with the dimming noise level—it's saying something I can't quite understand. "It feels different, too. Like something's calling to me."

"What do you mean?" My eyes flick up long enough to catch a shared look between my sister and her mate. *"A voice, or...?"*

"Like family, Sister." I'm nodding to myself. *"Yeah, like someone very important wants to say hello."*

"Wants to say hello..." I mutter this after erecting my shield, blocking everyone from hearing me. Everyone but her as I recognize what that sensation was then and now.

It's connected to this fae woman somehow. To the same aura currently petting and stroking across my limbs, burning me from the inside out as it's done all these years.

Back then, it was a light, innocent touch. A warmth that accompanied me every single day. At all times. Nothing sexual, but always comforting—soothing the hole left behind by my parent's death.

I'm given a taste of love with it as a beautiful pair of eyes appear before my closed ones. They're violet and a little large—an air of innocence in them that makes me smile—but what warms my chest and causes my cock to give a sharp throb is the slow flutter of her long lashes.

It's always been her.

In my thoughts. A connection that's grown over the last century, but demanded my attention these last few weeks.

How is this possible? She wasn't alive then...

Yet one look into her warm, violet eyes, and my world stops. She's where I begin and now end—the prize at the end of my battles. Who I will kill for.

It's a silent vow as fighting breaks out between the fae royals and my family. They fall one by one while my attention remains focused on my female, barely giving those left standing a glance before returning once again to her expressive eyes. They too bounce between me and the scene before us, watching as her king and his son are left for last, but as Larue is dealt a final blow by an angry god, two men approach my reason for existing. A step at a time, they encroach on her shivering form—forcing her back a few steps, but I'm between them before either man can lay a hand on her.

A royal general and the fae prince; both are surprised to see me when I return to my flesh form as another scream rends the air seconds later, and this time, it's from a female. My sisters are safe and my family is at peace, but the same cannot be said for the bloody corpse a few feet from Isabella. The sight alone is gruesome, a bit disturbing, and the guard with the shaved head calls out the name *Lilou* a second before the back of his knees are kicked and he drops to the ground.

Those with us are quick to subdue him and Prince Ruben, shackling both while I turn to look at the fragile doll I'll one day claim.

She's simply beautiful. Delicate.

Battling between relief and her grief, she teeters on shaky legs.

And the part of me programmed to protect her reignites with a burning urgency that causes every muscle in my body to contract and flex, bringing me just another step closer. I don't stop until I'm standing within reach. An inch or two of space is all I allow between us, and I tip her face up with the pads of two fingers while my other hand grips her hip to steady her.

Electricity sparks where I touch her, my cock throbbing as I get the first taste of her lithe form within my hold. Even through layers of clothing, I feel her. The delicious curve of her childbearing hips and the flash of heat coming off her skin as the scent of strawberries and cream deepens with a rich note of caramel.

It's a sugary-sweet and buttery combination. Makes my mouth water as pearls of pre-come slip from my dick while those expressive eyes darken a little.

Motherfuck, her arousal will forever be my weakness. I want to bathe in this heady perfection.

"W-Who are you?" She's a little breathless now and blushing from the tips of her pointed ears to the swell of her chest. So fucking sweet.

"Hello, little mate."

CHAPTER 2
Anaya

TWO WEEKS BEFORE THEY MEET...

"**Y**our Highness, I'd like to request an audience." My voice carries throughout the busy dining room, causing those eating to pause mid-bite and simultaneously turn their heads in my direction. They don't see how nervous or jittery I am—how I'm failing to hide my unease as the weight of their attention makes my skin crawl and the tips of my pointed ears flush. Nor do they acknowledge the slight shaking in my tone and the nasty glower sent my way from their beloved prince.

All they recognize is my audacity…

I'm supposed to be seen and not heard as I'm being fed a few pieces of lettuce with a slice of toast while they feast like gods. I'm supposed to be admired because of my title, but never more than that, just as my mother was during the end of her reign.

I'm an object the king parades in front of the fae court to appease their curiosity. To them, we're the picture-perfect family. To them, our strong bond and strict moral compass are admirable, but it's all a lie. There's no happiness or peace, much less affection within these castle walls.

You are nothing but a pawn I move at my discretion. You have no voice or choice; remember that, my child.

It's a lesson drilled into me since birth by my father; a princess can never step out of line. She is bound by duty: to her people and her king—their demand for compliance is silent, yet the threat ripples loud and clear over me by those whose blood runs through my veins every single moment of the day.

I'm hated by the two men these people adore because I'm a woman.

I'm scared of the punishment they'd inflict, but that's a matter our king will always handle privately.

He'd never do anything to tarnish his reputation in front of the few elders accompanying us, something my brother, Ruben, doesn't approve of. It's there in his expression, the intimidating way he leans forward in my direction while puffing out his chest to make himself appear bigger. A complex he's had since before my birth—since the day King Astor clipped his wings, and then the vampire king's trusted snake guard dragged him back to our kingdom.

They've grown back, of course, but not correctly. Jagged and a bit lackluster while molting at a near-constant pace, almost as if cursed. And being an injured fae—having that sacred piece of you taken is the most heinous and heartbreaking thing—it's only fueled his black heart.

My brother has learned no lesson; a complaint these elders hold over his head when talks of succession are brought up. I wasn't there that day, born nearly a century later, but the story has been carried on and shared by everyone who works in this castle.

By the very men surrounding us at this table.

"Sister, how dare you—"

"What's this about, Anaya?" Father says, interrupting our prince. Both men are watching me, matching eyebrows raised now while drumming their fingers atop the glass tabletop in a three-beat sequence that makes my legs shake beneath the cover of the ostentatious piece of furniture we sit at.

I know that count. It's their preferred punishment countdown: a 3, 2, 1 cadence before the sharp strike of a whip—physically or by Father's aura—or an open palm across my face.

I've felt that sting in the past. Many times. For any indiscretion or simply because of my father's distrust.

Because the fae king considers my words to be an insult to his position.

Swallowing hard, I square my shoulders and try to settle myself. My hands shake and I'm quick to lower them, placing each palm facing down atop my dress-covered thighs. The fabric is ruched and itchy, something not from this era, and I hate it.

All of this. All of them.

"I'd like to discuss something of great importance, Your Highness." Although I fail at keeping my tone unaffected, I meet his stare head-on. For the first time in years, I don't look down and silently implore him to listen. I pray he grants me the chance to plead my case—to try to use the mental link he leaves open from time to time between us. *Please, Father. I do not wish to marry—*

"Say it out loud, Daughter." His eyes narrow and his jaw ticks, showing his displeasure in the most innocuous way. A norm for him in front of the elders here, making the members of the fae court believe that while stern, their king isn't a monster.

They see him as a visionary and prophet. A man unafraid to fight and whose words hold more weight than those of the gods.

Yet he's much more than that.

Roi de cons: he's the king of idiots.

An opportunist who used his forced bond with the true queen, his chosen mate, and stripped her of everything. Her reputation, her self-respect, and then her life were all taken by him. Because of his abuse and neglect. Because of his greed.

My father.

The Fae King.

Our destruction.

His subjects don't realize the evil that lurks behind his eyes. This man is a thief, liar, and beyond cruel.

Clearing my throat, I give him a respectful bow of the head. Stay that way until he clears his throat, allowing me to continue now that he's somewhat appeased by the show of loyalty to his crown. "My king, I'd like to discuss my future with you. That, and my mate."

"What *mate* do you speak of?" His voice is low and unaffected, yet it hits me like a punch to the gut. Years ago, I'd felt this unexplainable pain in my chest that none of our mages could find a reason for. It ached for days, leaving me gasping for breath while deep bruising appeared near my lower ribs and stretched to just beneath my right breast. Our female healers tried to find its origin, but then it all disappeared. The deep ache. The discoloration of my flesh. Just gone. "Yours is dead, Anaya. You know this."

Audible gasps follow that statement as if they didn't know, but I don't react to the lies. Instead, I fight back the urge to rub a hand over my aching heart, where the absence of a mate I'll never meet throbs.

Not that it would gain me an ounce of empathy from these people. If anything, I'd be seen as trying to manipulate through sympathy because women can never be fully trusted. We're an emotional and argumentative sex—the catalyst and downfall of so many species.

It's a lie fed to keep us out of power.

Proves just how much men like my father fear losing control.

Taking in a deep breath, I let it out slowly while embracing the feelings coursing through me. There's this bone-deep exhaustion, while at the same time, I'd like to burn this castle to the ground. I don't, though. If anything, I merge the two and punish myself so that my ire doesn't hurt those who are innocent.

I may not be tall or even have muscles like most of those here, but my powers are more than enough to protect me—but at what cost? If my father knew I could control the element of water, I'd be used in his never-ending quest to rule over all beings. If he knew I possessed healing abilities, I'd become his forced servant to ensure his immortality.

He'd hurt my people to subjugate me.

Two things I can never allow. I'd rather let him think me useless than show my hand.

My mother knew this before her death and made me promise to never show my gifts.

At least, not until I met him. My mate.

He's dead, Anaya. You'll never know what it's like to wake up in his arms or feel completely safe. I'm not trying to look pitiful, but acknowledging this makes my bottom lip tremble. "I understand, Father. It's a pain that cuts my soul deeply."

"Then why do you insist?"

"Because I will always love the man—"

"Emotions are a weakness, Anaya. You know this."

"They're also the biggest motivator." The words are out of my mouth before I can bite each back, and he's angered by them. There's a harder clenching of his jaw and his aura darkens, forcing many in the room to do as I did and bow their heads. Something he pulls back from quickly.

Those under his doctrine aren't blind to his true nature; our guards are as corrupt and black-hearted, wanting to eradicate anyone and anything that isn't of fae blood. They know he's a violent man, his crimes, but not his dignitaries—the eldest among our kind have been glamoured to believe him just and righteous. He has plenty of dark magic mages to make it so, and it's something he can't afford to have undone. His image cannot crumble.

My eyes sweep across the table, and I catch more than a few questionable expressions, especially from my maternal grandfather who sits beside my intended, not understanding what just happened.

Is he truly unaware my mate is dead? That I'm being forced to marry a man I loathe?

A royal guard with greedy aspirations and an empty soul. I've seen Brice abuse those of lower rank—men and women who work inside these castle walls. A kick, a slap, and once, he whipped a first-year recruit who asked a question during his orientation.

He's always made his desire to own me known—a wife he can subjugate and use to rise higher in rank.

"My apologies." My father stands from his seat, the legs of his high-back, tufted chair scrapping harshly over the all-white flooring. It's loud against the marble, more than likely leaving a smudge behind that a maid will later clean before his next meal. "This is a personal matter, and I must attend to my daughter's distress. Please excuse us; I'll be retiring to my office now. Anaya, please follow me."

"Yes, my king." Before the last word has left my lips, every person stands and gives another bow. This one is deeper; they nearly fold themselves in half and completely ignore my scared expression.

Everyone except my brother and my betrothed, who turn their heads in my direction. Their matching amusement causes a shiver of fear to run down my spine; I'm caught between a flight or fight instinct that loosens the tenuous hold on the powers I have.

They flicker inside of me. Become a warm ripple down my limbs until they settle on my spread fingertips. The move is instinctual, and it's not until the cup in front of Ruben tips over and onto his plate, the water inside ruining his meal, that I force my hands into tight fists. It serves to create the distraction I need as he yells out, calling for a maid to clean the mess.

He's frustrated while the rest of our guests look his way, including Brice.

No one knows it's me, but the murmur inside starts at once. I'm blamed, not for the action but because of this being a direct result of the king's displeasure with my outburst.

I've never seen His Majesty so upset.

Princess Anaya should be grateful for his interference.

Brice is a wonderful young man. Stepping in to take care of my mateless—

Not wanting to risk another mistake, I exit the room before my grandfather finishes speaking. It hurts more coming from him. To know he thinks my abuser and future warden is a blessing.

Anaya, I do not like to be kept waiting.

Father's voice rips through my head, and his fury isn't veiled. The painful mental stab causes a yelp to escape me as my body titters. I'm not far from him, but I have to pause a second or two while using the wall for support. It's one of the gifts he's been born with, the ability to communicate with anyone or any species through a mental link he creates at will.

My apologies, Father. Just stopped to wash my hands.

Something most people don't know about him: King Larue is a stickler for etiquette and rules. Respect, behaviors, and hygiene—the latter of which he's a bit compulsive about.

You have three minutes.

Thank you.

Using the half bath a few doors before reaching his office, I slip inside and make quick work of washing and then drying my hands before rushing out. I'm still a bit weak after the mental attack, my head throbbing now, but I can't afford to take a moment and relieve my pain.

Instead, I take in measured breaths with each step toward his open door, not pausing but choosing to silently walk in and stop in front of his desk. The large mahogany piece takes up a large section of this room along with the floor-to-ceiling shelves lined with books on our history and that of other species.

Minutes tick off the clock while he ignores me, reading a page from an old and very thick book. The outside is bound by weathered leather and holds the royal fae symbol at the center, his finger lazily sweeping across the tree of life within a golden circle.

I make the mistake of exhaling roughly and his head snaps up, true fury in his eyes. "I'm being very patient with you, my daughter. What you did out there was not only disrespectful to me, but to Brice as well. He is to be your husband, Anaya. You owe him a great deal of gratitude."

"Gratitude?" The word feels wrong. Nearly makes me express my disgust, but I manage to hold myself back by digging my nails into the palms of my hands. This—the very idea of giving myself to anyone who isn't my mate—goes against every fiber of my existence. Makes me sick, and I fight back the feeling while his aura attacks mine. It's like the strike of a snake's sharp fangs lashing against my torso until I release a low whimper and drop to my knees. "I'm sorry."

"You will be if you ever embarrass me again." He's angry, his tone barely containing the ire he's directing at me. The tethers of his magic continue to punish me as if they were the leather strap of a belt, bathing me in pain without a single welt being left behind. "You will do as you're fucking told. Is that clear?"

Why do you hate me?

Not that I look up from my position; I keep my eyes down while another set of feet stop next to me. They're big and covered by a pair of black boots that belong to our military's uniform. Then, there's the scent of sardines that comes from him. It's unpleasant and something I loathe, but at the least, Father has stopped punishing me.

Why is he here? What are they—

The clearing of a throat snaps me back into focus, two people now standing over me. My father and Brice. Both hovering, their stares unnerve me, but I remember what they're waiting for.

"Yes, Father."

"Good." A heavy hand pats my head, the cool, thick band of a gold ring slightly knocking my scalp. "And you will never bring up this foolishness again. Right, Anaya?"

"Please, my king. Please hear me out."

The fingers atop my head grip my hair and yank my head back, forcing my eyes to his. My father glares while tears gather in my eyes from the sting. "I will be benevolent and give you this one chance to speak your piece. You have two minutes."

"Please don't make me marry someone who's not my mate."

"He is dead, Anaya. You know this; I told you he must've passed away from sickness or while serving in my army. So many casualties have befallen us over the last century."

Over a war he started. But I don't say this out loud, choosing to exhale slowly. "My heart hasn't healed. I feel lost and empty, need—"

"She can be given some time, my king," Brice interjects, cutting me off while my father forces my head in the guard's direction. To anyone else, he'd come off as understanding, but this isn't a man who does anything without gaining something in return. "I'll grant my darling princess this concession, but it will come with a steep condition."

No one says anything for a few minutes after that, yet I'm still forced to meet Brice's eyes. Eyes that taunt me, their natural color growing darker as he enjoys the view of me on my knees and help-less. They roam over my figure, lingering a bit longer on the exposed cleavage of my old-fashioned dress before tilting his head to the side.

And father lets him as if I'm owned already.

"Anaya. Answer him."

"What is the price I must pay, Sir Brice?" Low, and yet my tone reverberates as if I'd shouted my answer from the castle's rooftop.

"You must wear my ring."

Swallowing hard, I nod. "Can it be on a chain?"

"As long as it remains on your body, I do not have a preference, Anaya. Do you agree?"

"I do."

"Good. Then you will start now." Brice dips a hand into his front trouser pocket and pulls out a small velvet-covered box. It's old and worn, the outside hiding a piece of jewelry that's beautiful, but wrong. More so when he removes a chain from around his neck and slips the ring through it before placing it around mine.

A literal collar.

A sentence of condemnation.

"Well done, Brice. I approve of this union wholeheartedly."

"That means a lot, my king."

"What do you think, Daughter? Will you now cease this idiotic behavior…?" The *or else* silently hangs in the air, and instead of being given a chance to answer, I'm rewarded with another one of his attacks. A single lash lands right across where the atrocity sits on my neck, the pain forcing me to bite the inside of my cheek until it bleeds, but I don't dare make a sound. "Are you satisfied, or do we need to baby another of your tantrums?"

They both look at me expectantly, as if I haven't been abused.

"I am happy. Truly so." Through gritted teeth, I manage the words *and* keep my voice as soft as possible. "Thank you for being so understanding."

"Always, my child." He gives one last tug on my hair before the locks are released and I can move my neck a bit. Enough to ease the mounting crick there. "Now. I'll leave you two alone to talk."

Immediately after that, Father takes a step away from us, and then another while heading toward his office door. He doesn't look back or ask me to stand, much less warn Brice not to touch me—my nerves are fragile and shaken before the soft thud of both doors closing follows.

"You embarrassed me, ma princesse. Your denial won't end well for you."

"Is that a threat?" He extends a hand to help me stand, but I ignore it after that statement. My knees hurt—my entire body throbs, but I'll never accept help from this man. No matter how much I teeter on my heels or how I shake from the pain, I'd rather eat iron than touch him willingly. "I don't need your help."

"Yet one day soon enough, you'll beg me for it."

"I won't." Resolute. A bit of my power comes through each word, but the leering smirk on his face tells me he doesn't sense it. That, or I'm so far beneath him, he'll never see me as a real threat. "I vow this."

"Then I foresee a lot of pain in your future, Anaya." With the tip of two fingers, he traces across one cheek and then the other before tapping me on the nose. "I'll make you bleed on my cock and then force you to lick it clean afterward. I'll fuck you in front of the entire royal court and tell your father it's a punishment for disobedience, and he'll allow it, might even clap me on the back because you are beneath us."

Every part of my being wants to curl in on myself. I'm repulsed and scared and willing my trembling limbs to settle and not serve him this victory on a proverbial silver platter. Because this is what they want. My compliance and abject horror—to force me into playing whatever role they see fit and they wish.

So I swallow back the sob that's building inside my chest.

I force myself to meet his stare, unwavering in my stance.

"You're a pig. All of you are."

This causes him to laugh, loud and boisterous. Brice looks at me as if I were the stupidest yet cutest thing he'd ever seen. "And you'll fall in line, Anaya. Don't make me hurt you, because I promise you, I'll take great pleasure in your destruction. Play your part, and never embarrass me again." The way his expression softens then scares me more than his words. It's eerie—unnerving how easily he can threaten me with rape and then act as if he truly has feelings for me. "I care for you, Princesse. Always have. Why can't you see that? Why force me to be cruel?"

"You're not my mate."

"Yet once you bear my mark, I'll be your everything."

"What about the day you meet your mate? Think about them—"

"I'll kill anyone to claim what belongs to me, Anaya. My own family if it ever came to it." There's no mistaking how serious he is, the depth of his greed and the atrocities he's willing to commit in order to mate with me.

He's a true monster, and I need to escape this palace before that day comes.

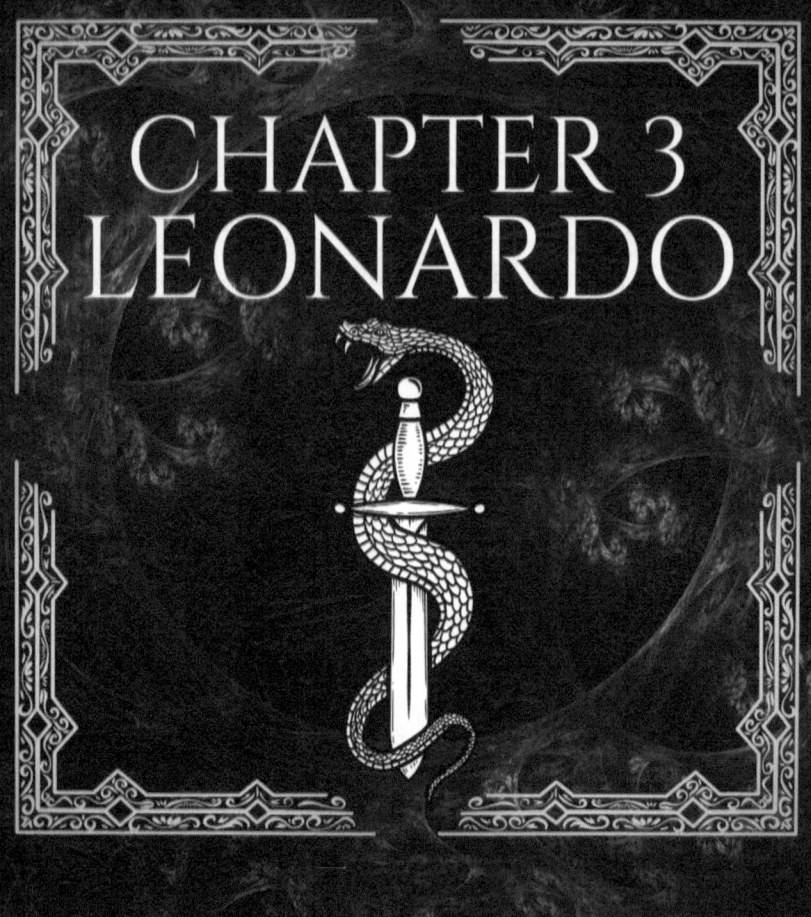

CHAPTER 3
LEONARDO

"How the fuck did she vanish into thin air?" I hiss out, staring into the worried face of my general and friend. Augusto's served the Moore house for over two centuries now and protected my mother long before her offspring became his sole mission, but more than that, he's someone I value and trust, as does everyone under my aegis. "Has anyone been able to scribe Silla's location? There has to be a trail we can follow."

It's been almost a week since her disappearance. A hundred and forty-eight hours since my aunt crossed our royal lands and trekked into unclaimed territory, wanting to forage a specific type of herb used in her daily evening tea. Something she could easily grow here, but Aunt Silla refuses to use anything that isn't grown wild and unattended. Moreover, this isn't the first time she's ventured deeper into the forest and past my kingdom; it's a routine every third day of the new month after she reinforces her barriers with a combination of black salt and mugwort.

To keep her strong. To keep her hidden from her mate and to break their connection, even though he's never shown his face after almost killing her.

This time, though, Silla's whereabouts are untraceable and the guard accompanying her was found unconscious—paralyzed from the neck down with traces of a poisonous powder surrounding his bulky frame. Both cases have left little to no evidence behind to work with, a heavy weight on my shoulders and chest cutting deep as I've failed them.

These two witches are under my protection.

He's loyal and smart; a younger warlock with the gift of olfactory, unlike anything I've ever seen. His tracking abilities and knowledge of terrains are why I trusted him with her care. And Silla, she's like a mother to me. Loved and took care of me all these years as if I were her offspring, and the knowledge I failed her weighs heavy on me. My heart feels tight, the organ throbbing with a mixture of pain and shame.

I've been blind, and the stench of betrayal is growing…

"No, my king. I'm sorry." Augusto's frown deepens, a heavy exhale escaping him while he spreads another map atop my desk. This region in Italy is one I'm all too familiar with and have avoided for over a century. There's nothing left for the Moore family there. "We've scoured every inch of the territory and have reached out to a few of the neighboring covens, but no one has seen her. Not even her friend. That old healer from—"

I'm shaking my head before he's done speaking. "She wouldn't contact anyone from Naples. Since Uncle Roberto's deception, those lands bring her nothing but heartache, even if the worst of his betrayal happened in this house."

"His actions hurt everyone. All Wiccan across the world, but none more than Silla," he replies while busily crossing out areas we've already searched and drawing circles over those I'll be personally visiting soon. However, my eyes haven't shifted from the area Silla once shared with her mate. Our uncle will always be remembered as a disgrace. It's a stain on my family's name, yet the house remains intact at her sentimental request.

The *why* never made sense; I would gladly destroy it.

"Have there been any new threats against Silla lately?"

"Only the ones you know about. Then, there are the two drugged witches we caught trespassing and are still under custody. I'm not sure about those two…"

"Something doesn't add up here." We'd found them under some weird hallucinogenic. Talking nonsense and demanding to speak to their king who was already standing in front of them. I've kept them in separate holding rooms since then, monitoring their progress, but so far nothing. "Are they still unresponsive?"

They've remained ignorant. Or are they playing so?

I need to make a trip to their cells.

"And the others?"

"You're aware of the small unrest within the younger generations of certain covens. Young witches that blame Roberto for the deaths of their ancestors, but none have acted upon their threats. Especially not after your recent visit."

I nod, raising a brow. "Do you trust them? Think any of them are connected to this?"

"It's a mostly harmless group of young Wiccans just testing boundaries." He looks up and smiles, meeting my eyes. "More than likely, they just wanted to meet their king. They idolize you."

The small jibe pulls a chuckle from me, but it doesn't last long. Over the last few weeks, I've spoken to and blessed many of the Wiccan territories he's speaking of. I've given them my support—

helped heal those who hold on to the pain of loss and who need guid-ance to move on—and while many have accepted my help, one coven isn't bending the knee.

I'm once again reminded of the sour taste left in my mouth after meeting with two of the original surviving Rossi clan members; a female cousin of the former elder and his youngest daughter who were out of the country during the near extermination of their blood-line by my brother-in-law, the vampire king.

Instead, these two females want a union between our families, not believing that their ancestors caused the death of our former king and queen. And as the new monarch, I find their stance insulting.

The youngest sibling of Lilibeth, both my sister's friend and our greatest betrayer, was but a few months old at the time. For most of her life, she's stayed away but has cultivated an infatuation that will never be reciprocated. She isn't my mate, and I'd never touch a female that isn't mine—born from the other half of my soul to fill that which has been left vacant.

To take a chosen mate or fuck another woman is a sin.

"Chiara will be a problem." Running a hand down my face, I grit my teeth. "She's entitled and self-centered and I have no patience for her insolence."

"Should we contact Christopher? He's their elder now." An old warlock, he was spared on the day of the great massacre and told to run. Theodore let him live. Mercy was shown to an innocent young witch back then, and he'd done just that by keeping what was left of their clan in line. They've given me no problems over the years, but times change.

Newer generations with ideas of grandeur have emerged, and my patience is thin. More so when it comes to the very memory of these traitors I watched that day from a hidden nook inside a hollow oak that still stands inside our property line as the Rossi members took great joy in killing my father and then dragged my mother over his brutalized corpse.

I had a good view of the manor's front door, even if I had to contort myself a bit to see. Isabella hid me there in her rush to find our sister—forgetting that small detail—with a protective spell warding off any threat, but more importantly, no one outside my family could sense my location.

"Long live our king! Long live our king!" a male voice shouted with glee, the sadistic tone of the Rossi clan's leader carrying throughout our lands, and those with him joined in on the mocking chant. They laughed while feet stomped the ground, the horde shaking the very soil they stood upon, and I felt the vibrations from my hidden prison.

My eyes snapped open then, and I bit down on my bottom lip until it bled, gnawing at the flesh until I knew a permanent scar would be left behind as a reminder of this night.

There were so many witches here, and they all smelled of rotting flesh. This acrid perfume permeated every inch of these lands as they dragged my father out our front door while down on his knees. He didn't fight back or challenge their magic, letting them brandish attacks like whips that burned his body from different angles.

Our king's blood stained the floor. My father's pain was palpable.

And yet, when his head rose and his eyes met mine inside the tree a final time, all I could feel was his love. His absolute pride and faith in knowing we'd protect our people and then avenge his death after securing our future. It was all there in his soft smile and the nod sent my way, an action none of his executioners saw right before he mouthed the words: close your eyes, son.

And a second after I did, my father was gone.

I felt it. His death.

This painful tear in my soul as our familial bond was brutally ripped from me, leaving behind a gaping wound. Everything hurt. To breathe or move or cry—it took everything inside me not to release the untrained and a bit hostile magic that resided within me at the time, but then I remembered his words...

Volatile emotions are uncontrollable and will kill you from within.

I couldn't destroy the sacrifice he and my mother so unselfishly made for their children and our future generations.

I lost a part of me that night, and only my fated mate would make me whole again. It's a day I abhor and long for in the same breath. She'll always be a reminder of my past while also serving as a balm to soothe and patch the cracks left behind.

"Yes. Arrange a meeting in San Lucido three days from now."

"Any place in particular?"

"We'll phone him the location and time the night before and warn him to come alone. Total discretion." San Lucido isn't near his home or my forest, but close to a grouping of smaller covens that reside near the Italian coast and who know my aunt well, and right now, she's still my main priority. "Something's wrong, Augusto. I can feel it—this prickling of foreboding has been growing over the last few weeks, and I'm restless. Since before our last visit to were-wolf territory."

"What do you sense? Does it have anything to do with Silla's insistence with Isa?"

He—everyone—was put off by my aunt's need to speak with my sister. They find it pushy, while I thought it necessary, but now I'm wondering…

Did Silla know she'd be taken?

Did she want help from Isabella?

Nodding, I turn and walk over to the floor-to-ceiling windows inside my study and take in the beauty of our lands. This forest is lush and dense, vast beyond what the eye can see, and brimming with secrets that few are privy to.

There's also a deep connection between us; a link—to each towering tree and the bright green moss that decorates each thick and gnarled trunk—that's ever alive inside my chest. I feel the sway of each leaf as if it were my limb. I enjoy the warm sun as it heats these grounds and the heavy scent of damp soil and blooming wildflowers that perfume my home.

Then there's the people and fauna that thrive here. From witches to animals, we're united by an intricate ecosystem, and I'm humbled to be their king.

Taking in a deep breath, I let it out slowly as I listen to an ancient song that not many are privy to. Most species alive aren't, but I can make out the low cadence of every rustle or chirp and then the low hum of those souls who died here.

Not like Gabriella and her gift, the ability to give and take a life, but more of an acknowledgment of the magic that dwells on these lands.

"Utter devastation and then peace."

"My king, I do not understand. What does that mean?"

"Neither do I." It's the truth. The two emotions are contradicting, on opposite sides of the spectrum, and I've yet to decipher if this is an inclination of what's to come. *I need to speak with Isabella. Maybe she's seen something?* "Truth is, I'm at odds with myself and not much is making sense, Augusto. Yet, I—"

The pounding of feet rushing in our direction stops me seconds before there's a sharp knock at the door. I'm already turning toward the entrance, as is Augusto, when the voice of an older witch, a female I've hired to help me run the house, filters through the wooden structure.

"Your Majesty, I'm sorry to interrupt, but King Evergreen's on the phone. He says it's urgent." She's agitated. Her worry is palpable through the tremble in her tone. "He's called five times now."

I don't bother replying and walk to the door, opening it while holding out my other hand for the mobile. I'd left my cell phone with her earlier today, asking not to be disturbed unless an emergency or word of Silla came through.

"Thank you, Isotta."

"Of course, my king." Nodding, she scrunches her brows. Her worry lines are thick after handing the device over and then stepping back. "I'll bring up your coffee and cake now."

Not that she gives me a chance to refute. Isotta's gone before I bring the phone up to my ear. Yet when I do, I hear it. There's a pain-filled sound that causes my heart to clench. "Brother? What's wrong?" Augusto comes closer then, his head inclined a bit. I'm sure he's trying to pick up bits and pieces of what Xadiel's saying, the general's aura tumultuous with worry, but right now that takes a back seat to the anguish of my brother-in-law's wolf. His low howls are heartbreaking. "Xadiel, talk to me. Are you okay? Isa?"

"She's gone." It's a garbled sound. More animal, than man. "I need you to come home."

"What do you mean *gone*? Where's my sister, Brother?"

"With Larue." Two words are all it takes for a visceral rush of ire to run through every inch of my over six-foot frame. There's no one in this world I despise more than the fae king. I want his head on a pike outside my bedroom window. I will cleanse the world of his filth—sanctify our future by ridding the world of the entire royal fae bloodline.

"How?" It's grit out, the phone in my hand cracking in my hold. Small shards of glass hit my skin, leaving a trail of small cuts behind on my cheek that slowly began to bleed. I feel the few drops as they roll down my flesh and then onto my clothes, ruining the white t-shirt I'd put on this morning before training.

"He cut her where she's the weakest. The arsehole threatened those—"

"She loves most," I interject, finishing for him. Because if there's one thing Isabella is, it's unselfish. Giving. Honest. My sister carries the weight of the world on her shoulders silently to protect us, and I can't be mad at her for this because I trust her.

Isa saw this. Of that, I'm sure.

"…come home, Leo. I need your help."

"I'll be there in a few hours, brother. Keep the faith." From the corner of my eye, I catch Augusto grabbing a small wooden chest from the shelves to my right. He doesn't open it—can't as it's sealed and only to be unlocked by those of Moore bloodline—and then places it atop my desk. The general doesn't speak but puts a closed fist over his heart before moving a few paces back and then taking a soldier's stance. Immobile. Waiting for orders. "She'd never will-ingly let herself be captured if she wasn't sure it was the right thing to do, Xadiel. You know Isa loves you and would never leave you without just reason."

"That's what her first letter said." There's a hint of wistfulness in his tone, but that soon changes to desperation. Those two can't be without each other. Their connection rivals the one my parents had, a deep and all-consuming true mates' bond. "That I'd soon know what to do."

"Do you trust her?"

"I do. With my life."

If there's a man in my life—people I respect—it's them. Isabella and Xadiel have always been there for me and stepped up in what-ever capacity I needed growing up. Made sure that I never missed out. Even now, my sister and her mate are closer to me than anyone.

Moreover, the only other person I consider a parental figure is missing, too.

Each one of them stepped in and took care of a teenager who at times was lost and alone. They taught me in their own way to control my anger when all I wanted to do was lash out.

"You said the first letter?"

"The second needs deciphering. It's in an ancient language I'm not familiar with, but you and Gabriella are." There are voices around him, familiar ones I'm picking up on now, and I understand where he is. He's gone to get help from my other sister and her mate, a vampire with underworld connections. "We'll be back on my lands tonight. We're leaving Seattle now."

"And I'll meet you there, then. I'm coming."

"Thank you." This time, the reply sounds more like him. His beast is stepping back, and it's an honor to know I'm someone Xadiel trusts. "Too many days have passed since her disappearance and I'm—we're—not handling this well. My beast and I need her back in our arms."

My brows furrow. "How long has she been gone, Xadiel?"

"Five days today."

One less than Silla.

Goddess, please tell me this is a coincidence. "She's not the only one missing," I say, and my voice wavers as I do. That feeling of foreboding I've been battling against causes every muscle in my body to clench, the pain rippling through my chest. "We can't find her."

"Who? Who's missing?"

"Aunt Silla."

"How long has she been missing, Leo? Why didn't you call me?"

"Six days, and we've been looking for her. Thought she might've taken some time for herself since the anniversary of Roberto's—"

"Do you think it's related? That they're together?" His tone is sharp and the questions straightforward; this is the wolfen king speaking and not someone I consider my kin. Not that I don't under-stand; I'd react the same way if it were my mate one day. The impor-tance of protecting, honoring, and cherishing your female is ingrained in our DNA since we're old enough to comprehend our laws.

No matter the species, mates are sacred.

"I don't think they're together. Why would he want Silla, too? She's of no importance."

"Yet I don't believe in coincidences when it comes to that piece-of-shit king, Leonardo." He blames himself; it's there in his tone, although the crime falls on Larue's shoulders. The fae king has been behind all of our misfortunes—the pain and tears shed—and he will pay for each one with his blood and that of his family.

So mote it be.

Aunt Silla's my responsibility out of gratitude and a familial bond, but my sisters come first.

Just as Isabella is Xadiel's world. Like Gabriella is the heart and soul of a vampire half-god.

The day my sisters set off to find their mates and form an alliance —provide the protection our sacred lands needed—I accepted them without hesitation. Appreciate everything they've done, but now it's time for me to sacrifice.

They've each had a heavy price to pay for the safety of all Wiccans.

Moreover, I owe them more than anyone here.

My life. My crown. My loyalty.

I will find them. I will lay Larue's corpse at their feet.

"You're right, Brother. And I know where I'll start."

If those two witches in my prison know anything, I'll find out. And if they're involved in any way, I'll honor my family by bathing our sacred grounds in their blood.

CHAPTER 4
Anaya

My mother's garden is one of my favorite places and at night. It's magical, a true enchantment as the flowers sigh and perfume the air, inviting you to close your eyes and find respite after a tiring day. It's my solace after playing a role all day: the dutiful daughter without a voice or choice.

Because I have neither. Just like this isn't the first time I find myself out late and wandering, walking through the only place left in my mother's kingdom that holds a bit of her essence.

She's here in these flowers and the ground I walk on. Her ashes *laid to rest among her favorite things—the white lilies here bloom year-long without pause, and it's because of her.*

They repaid her kindness since she planted the first bulb.

These lands miss her and silently weep with me.

Because many think she died a happy queen and mate, but I knew the truth. Mother ran from my father once, before I was born, and was dragged back to fulfill her duties to him and her people under constant watch. Under duress and heartache. No one cared about her happiness within these walls except me. Not even her father saw her, never really looked past the fake smiles and stoic behavior, much like he doesn't with me.

"One day, I'll be free." At the center of the garden, there's a large fountain that never ceases to run, and I'm sitting against the side that faces away from the castle. Not that anyone comes in here. Most treat this place like a shrine to be admired from afar and never touched, something on nights like tonight I appreciate.

My body is sore.

My throat burns as if I were catching a cold.

It's why I take in deep breaths and close my eyes, letting the sweet fragrance from these blooms bring me comfort, but then the breeze suddenly sweeps past me, ruffling my long hair, and with it, there's something new. Warm. Rich. A bit of spice that has no reason for being among these floral notes.

Yet I don't reject it. If anything, my chest expands and I pull it in deeper.

"What is that?" And in any normal setting, I'd open my eyes and go investigate, yet I'm afraid to move. To lose this…whatever it is because I want more. To hold it closer. "Chocolate with cloves."

That's what it reminds me of.

Of a cold night and warm blankets while sipping hot cocoa and looking out onto the fae lands. Of happier times when I had someone to lean on. When I felt safe and free. Young and carefree.

Before I was old enough to be taught "lessons" or forced to comply.

A smile tugs at my lips then, and I slowly open my eyes and almost gasp, but not out of fear. Standing before me is a shadow watching me with the warmest blue eyes I've ever seen. There's no malice in them or his touch as it slowly reaches out and cups my face with one firm hand.

I shouldn't be able to feel its warmth, but I do.

I shouldn't be able to feel its sweet breath on my skin as it bends low enough to place a chaste kiss on the tip of my nose, but I do. It tickles a bit and I squirm, a giggle slipping through, and I'm gifted another small peck.

Just those two before those blues orbs dull and I feel a pang inside my chest. Sadness. Emptiness as the warmth from a second ago disappears along with the shadow, and behind it enters an arctic-like frost that makes me shake. My teeth rattle, but I hear it.

Faint.

A male voice.

"Soon."

I jolt in bed as the realization that I'm actually cold hits home. I'm freezing.

It's the kind of temperature drop that sets off alarm bells, unleashing the kind of bone-deep shivers and goosebumps that force me completely from my sleep. I come to almost painfully so, each sensation becoming harsher as the second tick by—the feeling settling deeper—and with it comes my complete alertness.

"It was just a dream," I mutter as other things become apparent, forcing me to push away the memory of my moonlit walk through the garden. There's time to decipher and question and even consider myself crazy, but now isn't the time. Not when I'm dealing with a different shock to my system; a knowing that I'm not home, and it's confirmed when I force my eyes to look around the room through a half-loopy yet sharp gaze.

I'm in a modern, yet simple bedroom that lacks the ostentatious decor my father insists of all his properties. That's another thing. I've never been here before.

Not my room. Not my bed.

"Goddess, where am I?" This isn't a place I recognize, and my skin prickles as anxiety slams in. At once, the rush of a million ants crawling under my skin begins, and a choking gasp gets stuck in my throat. A throat that's coated in a bitterness I can't quite place yet. "How did I get here?"

Nothing in this room is familiar to me; the style or layout and the sharp light coming from what looks to be a bathroom doorway not far from where I lay. Moreover, the last thing I remember is going to bed late after spending most of the day atoning for my sins against the crown. Embarrassing our father during an important meal with our elders would never be forgotten, and he's let me stew—walk on eggshells for days on end—until he was ready to deal with my insolence.

It was his word. His way.

And the king's reasonable punishment was misogynistic at its core. Meant to show me my place. For nearly ten hours, I'd been forced to kneel while facing the wall inside a special room designed to deal with the females of his family.

My mother suffered in that room. I have, too.

Made to quietly accept a physical strike of a belt or the lash of my father's powers, but this time, I experienced something more demeaning. Brice decided my fate. He gave me a glimpse of what my life under his heavy hand would be like after asking me to turn and face him...

DAY OF PUNISHMENT

...

"I'm going to give you a choice, ma princesse," Brice says from his seat across from me while my father and brother watch from the opposite side of the room. They're both wearing matching expressions: pride and amusement at my subjugation. Their auras are dark and oppressing, and I almost flinch back. It takes every bit of the strength I allow myself to access—use for protection—to hold me steady. "You can have five strikes by my hand on any body part of your choosing. Or would you rather have no food for a week?" He pauses then, tilts his head to the side, and then nods. Not once do his eyes waver from me; I can feel their heavy presence while I concentrate on a speck of dirt near the edge of a Parisian rug older than I am. Father would be furious if he knew it was there. That's what I hold on to, a way to ease my anger while focusing on his compulsive demands for cleanliness while the room around me seems to shrink and beads of sweat fall down my back. "Either choice will be respected, Anaya. Think of this as another gift from your intended."

Bile rises, and the taste nearly makes me gag, but I breathe through the nausea. Exhale slowly through the tumultuous emotions fighting for dominance with me, from ire to fear to a desperate need to defend myself, but doing so will hurt any chance of an escape in the future.

If my father knew of my powers, he'd never let me go. I'd be hunted.

It's that knowledge that has me lifting my head just enough to give Brice the smallest of smiles, ignoring the hiss of protest from my brother. Because to him, as a woman, I should never be allowed to meet a man's eyes.

He's a chauvinistic pig. Learned from his idol.

"Thank you." The words taste like dirt on my tongue, acrid and wrong. "May I have a minute to decide, please?"

"You may." Brice is leering down at me from his position, lip curling over his teeth while his stare darkens. I'm not an idiot. I'm aware of the position I'm in and the ideas floating through his mind, more so when his gaze rakes down my face and neck, stopping at the swell of my chest that's accentuated by another ridiculously frilly dress from over a century ago.

Father rarely allows us to use clothing that isn't from an era he considers to be the height of his reign—when he took control of all species— an empty accomplishment as he didn't eradicate those he feared. He's lied to those who blindly follow his doctrine and celebrate his legacy.

Mother, in her last days and through delirium, exposed so much of his betrayal. I'm alive and mostly unharmed because of her warnings.

"You have thirty seconds, my bride."

Five seconds pass before I decide, my throat bobbing harshly. "No food."

"Is that your final answer?"

"Yes."

"Have you eaten today?"

"I have." There's no point in lying when he was sitting across from me during breakfast. My meal might've been small, just a few pieces of fruit, but he saw. "Just breakfast."

"Then your punishment begins tomorrow. For now, you will be given tea and laid to rest."

No sooner does he make the decision than a maid walks in with a dainty porcelain cup with a flowery design on a polished silver tray. Steam billows from the top, and the aromatic scent of lavender and honey with a small touch of citrus makes my nose twitch pleasantly, my body leaning toward it as if I were being pulled. It's a combination I enjoy, this soothing blend bringing forth a warmth in me—reminds me of my mother—and these men know it.

Red flashes across my processors, a clear warning, yet it is snuffed out quickly.

PRESENT

...

They watched me drink it.

Every single last drop while looking more than pleased with themselves.

But then, that's all I remember. After that, it's all a muddled mess, and as I take in the bland room and overwhelming cold settling deep in my bones, I understand. Something in that drink put me to sleep, and the longer I'm awake, the harsher the taste in my mouth becomes—making me aware of their betrayal.

Brice knew it would. So did my father.

My only solace in this is that by tradition and law, I cannot be sexually touched before my wedding night. A trusted mage from my mother's reign, a woman who does what she can to protect me behind our king's back, would be the only one to perform the check to reaffirm I'm a virgin on my wedding day. She'd never truly touch or check me, but the rest of the royal fae court doesn't know this.

My only silver lining.

"How long was I out?" My whisper reverberates throughout the empty room, bouncing against bland walls and back to me. I'm still a bit lethargic and panicky yet, having a problem moving, but still, I manage to toss the thick quilt off and sit up. There's no heating in this room, the large stone fireplace dirty with soot and old, half-burned chopped wood while what appears to be vents atop the bed are closed.

The more I look around, the colder I become.

Yet, even as I start to shake, I find the simplicity comforting. Lovely, as I take account of the pristine white furniture and soft cream bedspread currently tossed toward the foot of the bed. One that I quickly pick up and drape over my shoulders as I shuffle on stocking-covered feet toward the room's door. I'm still in the clothes I wore the day of my punishment, the frilly light pink dress doing very little to help build any warmth, and I have no choice but to tap into my powers.

The ability to heal comes in various ways.

I can fix a wound or eradicate a sickness, and right now, it's helping me raise my inner temperature. It happens gradually as I close my eyes, taking in measured breaths as I concentrate on my core. With one hand, I hold on to the quilt, and with the other, I press the open palm against my abdomen.

Slow from disuse, my powers begin to throb beneath my skin,

and my hand vibrates as the first rush of warmth blooms across my limbs, pulling a deep sigh from me. I'm thawing and fast becoming less stiff, and I know that whatever they put in my drink is now completely out of my system.

That bitterness I'd awoken with is gone. So is my anxiety, which leaves plenty of room for my anger to take the forefront ahead of fear —it keeps me from losing control of my faculties and rational thinking.

Instead, I harness the urge to destroy this place and heal myself. Water can be harnessed from where I stand; I sense it inside the pipes hidden behind the walls or the cold that surrounds me, but I don't.

There will come a day I won't pull myself back, but it's not today.

I'm checking my aura while thinking and planning, tilting my head to the side as I search for any sign of life outside these walls. There's none. No noise. Which I find surprising, and when the tethers of my magic turn a pretty blue color, I walk toward the wooden entrance. The padding of my feet is loud inside the quiet room, quickly followed by the turn of the plain black doorknob, but it's my angry spitting of the word *fuck* that echoes, drowning out any other sound.

And thank the goddess there's no guard nearby or they'd know I'm awake.

"They've locked me in." Another hiss and I turn, making a quick sweep—search for a secondary exit—and coming up empty. There's nothing outside of the bathroom and a small window mounted to the right of the bed and I walk toward it, trying to reach the ledge by standing on the tips of my unprotected toes. It's higher than normal on the wall, way out of my reach, and its only usefulness is that of letting in some much-needed natural light. Not much with the prism-like film covering the glass panels, but it's better than nothing.

I've slept in nothing. Just four walls and a bed whenever a lesson needs to be taught.

"It could be worse," I mutter low, letting out a quiet huff while the open bathroom door pulls my attention once again. With each step closer, I realize that what I thought to be a turned-on lamp illuminating the space is a glowing orb. It's floating with just a few inches of space between it and the flat ceiling, casting a bit of warmth to the otherwise sterile space.

The en-suite is larger than I first thought, too.

The pristine white stone is everywhere; it's the sole source material in every feature. The tub, sink and countertop, cabinets...even the bench inside of a large, double-feature shower. Yet that's not what's pulling me in deeper. That glow is highlighting a section of wall beside the tub that had I not looked hard enough, I'd have missed the near seamless door in the same material as the rest of the room.

And the closer I walk toward the hidden door, the stronger his stench becomes. Light; a gentle sweep of something foul until I gag and stagger. It slams into me, causing my entire body to lose its equilibrium and grip the closest object to me, which is a half wall separating the toilet from the rest of the room.

There's a small yelp from me as the cold from the stone seeps in, damaging the warmth I've pulled from my core, but that takes a back seat when my name is called a few seconds later and heavy footsteps draw nearer. Bulky and ungraceful, the intruder meets me at the bathroom's entrance, and I fight the urge to retch as Brice smiles down at me.

He's been in here before.

He's who uses that secret doorway.

"Nice to see you awake, ma princesse." I want to respond, but all I can taste in the air is that awful sewage aroma this male fae carries with him. *Yet it's never been this bad. This acrid.* His scent has never been a pleasant one for me—no scent match between us—but this is different. Almost as if he's decomposing before my eyes, and yet as I use a tiny sliver of my powers, my tethers find nothing physically wrong with him to explain the dramatic change.

My father's trusted general and personal guard at times is healthy, all things considered.

It takes a moment and a few attempts at clearing my throat to dislodge his natural perfume for me to try to answer. "I-I'm... what...?" Shaking my head, I exhale roughly and run a hand down my face. "Where are we, Brice?"

"In Canada." Two words, and they caused everything around me to plummet, and that ice-cold dread I'd felt after waking nearly swallows me whole. I'm drowning. The breath inside my chest is a painful shard of betrayal and fear for everything that could've been done to me while asleep.

I've been drugged.

I've been taken from my home in France and kept locked inside of a room Goddess knows where.

I need to leave. Can't wait any—

My nose twitches then and the scent of jasmine infiltrates my senses, cutting off my panicked thoughts. It's floral and sweet, but more than that, it helps bring my world back into focus, giving me a bit of the comfort the shadow in my dream gave. Not the same, but enough that I'm able to take a moment and rationalize my next move.

There's a sense of belonging attached to it, too.

The same familial pull I've only encountered with one other person physically: my mother. And while I know it isn't her and it hurts, I still move toward the doorway where Brice stands. I no longer see or fear him. Instead, I walk past and straight toward the room's wide-open entrance. That's when I catch sight of a woman being carried past us, her eyes closed and body limp in the arms of a younger guard.

He's not one I'm familiar with.

His eyes meet mine for a brief second, and in them, I find no malice. Nothing but a true sense of loyalty.

"You reacted strongly toward the witch, ma petite princesse. Why?" Brice's voice comes from behind me, too close for comfort, and it's full of disgust. Accusations. For me? For her? I do not know, but then a second later, I'm caught off guard as a thick arm wraps around my midsection, pulling me almost flush against his much larger frame. "What did she do for you to rush past me like that? For you to want to be closer?"

Brice is jealous. It pours out of him, deepening his horrid scent.

"That's not it," I say, voice low and calm while everything inside of me is revolting at his touch. My insides shudder and my gut churns, nearly making me sick, but doing so is completely useless right now. He has the upper hand, and shoving him off harshly or punching him in the face won't help me or the witch beckoning me to find her. If anything, it will make this sick game more interesting to him. *Remain calm. He's coming soon.* Those five words filter through my head in a gentle, female voice. It's not mine. Not one I've heard before, yet it doesn't set off any alarms somehow. "How is that even possible?"

It's almost as if her spirit, her soul, is telling me to...*trust* her. And for some reason, I do. My body becomes lax just long enough for the brute fae behind me to ease his grip. For me to step forward and out of his embrace.

"How is what possible?" Brice's deep timbre snaps me into focus and I shrug, but he doesn't like that. I'm whirled around and gripped once again; this time, his hand finds purchase on my right hip. Tight and uncomfortable, his touch almost causes me to look up, but I bite the inside of my cheek instead. I close my eyes and cling to the reassurance those five words, for some odd reason, gave me. *Remain calm. He's coming soon.* "Answer me, Anaya. What did you mean?"

"Nothing." I'm avoiding his probing stare because I don't have an answer. Not one that makes a lick of sense. "Just don't understand why she's here."

"Try again." Fingers dig in deeper. They almost cause me to cry out. "Last chance. The truth this time."

"Please step back. I need space."

"Look at me."

Remain calm. He's coming soon.

Coming soon.

Soon.

Just like the shadow's whisper. That last word gives me the strength to take in a deep breath and let it out slowly, and only then do I do as he asks. There's darkness in those brown orbs, and they watch me with a sick mixture of hunger and distrust. "Why would I want to be near a woman I don't know? Especially a powerful witch at that."

"Are you scared, Anaya?"

"Because of my father, all Wiccans hate me. He put a target on my back."

His chuckle grates my nerves; I want to push him away. "That we can both agree on."

The heat from his hand grows, as does the pinch of his blunt nails breaking the skin at my hip. It stings. How he managed to cut through the fabric of my dress, I don't understand, but then I smell it: charred fabric. The textile beneath his touch is being singed as he digs in, tearing until it's flesh on flesh.

How is he doing this? Did he hide this ability from my father?

"Let. Go." It's a hiss dripping with my pain. My side hurts so bad. "Stop this."

"You have nothing to fear, ma princesse." Yet the threat is there. Unsaid but ever-present. "Never disobey me, and I'll protect you."

"Please stop." Two words, pathetic in my begging, but he eases the torture and removes his hand, only to bring those same fingers up to my chin. Tips it up with two heated digits and smiles. "Why are you doing this? Why do you want someone who doesn't want you?"

"Because I can." Honest. Unashamed. "It's a lesson I learned from the man you loathe more than me. One that will cost the life of our new prisoner."

Is that what this is? Do they plan to kill the woman?

"Why is she here, Brice? That was no ordinary witch."

"Isabella Moore is—"

"The Wiccan princess turned wolfen Luna?"

"You know?" There's a smidgen of surprise in his tone. Shows in the narrowing of his eyes. "Then I'm sure you understand why you're here?"

"I'm not hurting her. I refuse to."

Laughter, unadulterated and dark, filters throughout the room, tinging the space with his wickedness. Everything around me seems to accept his mood, the unleashing of his aura that overwhelms but doesn't overtake me. Instead, it attacks and tries to find weakened spots in my defenses, hitting me with the quick strike of what feels like the snap of rubber bands.

It stings but doesn't do any damage.

He's toying with me. Does he know of my powers?

"Your job is simple here, Anaya. Take care of that Luna cunt and do as I say."

"And if I refuse?"

"Don't ask questions you're not ready to hear the answers to."

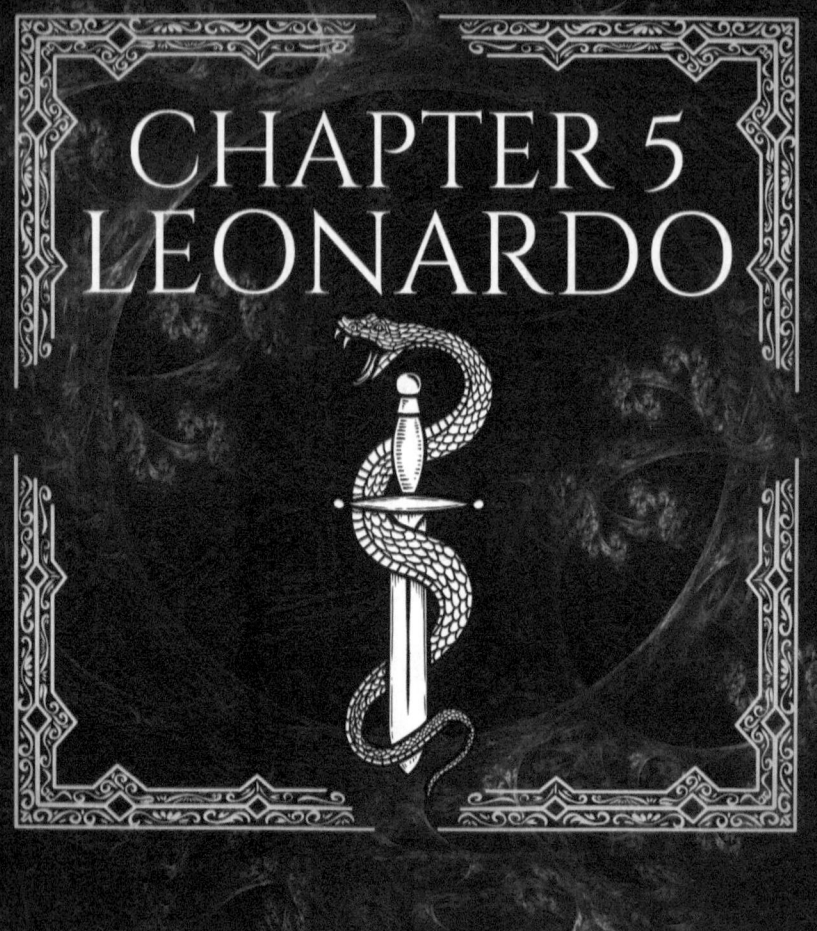

CHAPTER 5
LEONARDO

Out of the three kingdoms, I consider myself the more restrained ruler. Not passive or less lethal, but more like my father, who was feared because his strike, much like mine, is always meant to destroy. King Paolo Moore bestowed second chances and forgave until the last of his patience waned, and when it did, the prior Wiccan monarch was unrelenting in his pursuit of justice.

He craved peace and ruled much as I do, a man who values life, and that includes those outside of my aegis: werewolf, vampire, and witch alike. Even humans and then the merfolk who rarely leave their beloved sea. Every soul deserves a chance until proven unworthy to breathe.

My brothers-in-law don't always see it that way.

Theodore's always been bloodthirsty and unapologetic. Xadiel's dominant and brutal.

Myself, I've tried to keep my people at ease and the bloodshed to a minimum, until you touch someone I love. That's when the magic beneath my skin—the Moore blood in my veins heats—and I can no longer control the impulse to kill. Because it's there, just under control at all times. As king, I lead by example, more so as many of the surviving members of my coven have lived through the horrors of a massacre or the subjugation by those they trusted until my sisters saved them.

Moreover, those scars remain.

A century is nothing when compared to the memories ingrained into their beings.

What all witches and warlocks have endured to regain the sense of peace stolen by those led by greed and perverse needs. I made promises to rule fairly and stand by them. To protect my people, and that includes their mental health.

To end any and every threat that stands in my way, and right now, as I walk into the detention center where the two warlocks are being kept—cloaked by my powers—I find myself giving into those baser needs.

Earlier today, I found myself being tested.

I've also made peace with the fact I'm not so righteous after all, and have more in common with a bloodthirsty beast than I'd realized. Because I can taste it. I want their screams and agony. Their desperate pleas for the forgiveness I will never grant, and nothing else will suffice as I listen to their whispers from my place just a few feet from them. From where they sit completely unaware of my presence.

"We need to get out of here. This isn't what I agreed to," the blond, a warlock with ancient markings on his right arm—something akin to tattoos on his skin—whispers while the other man nods. He's older than he appears, more than my hundred and fourteen years, and it's in those lines embedded in his skin by charcoal ink that I'm able to decipher his possible age. The ritualistic symbols give away his origin.

The lines begin at just above the inside of his wrist and stop at the crook of his elbow, from thin to thickest, yet at the very center there's an all-seeing eye with long, well-pronounced lashes. This is the old marking for seers, though he's not one himself—of that, I'm sure.

Maybe it's an homage being paid. Or the wish for protection. However, what I'm most intrigued about is the iris, or lack of definition of one; the entire eye is black as midnight with not a single hint of a highlight or the white of a cornea to be found. Like a demon or shifted being, this is the eye of someone giving control to their *other* side.

It's also done to be feminine: maybe a deity's eye?

The entire piece holds a delicate touch. As if it was done with love.

How peculiar.

He's easily over two hundred years old, that much is clear to me, and from the Genoa region—a city not far from the French border and with an easy access point for the fae ruler. There are no covens there, all having moved away under threat of persecution and none ever returned, having settled closer to the San Lucido coast or these royal lands.

"I agree. Something isn't right." His companion is younger and looks rougher around the edges, too—a wanderer. And while there's nothing wrong with that—I respect the nomad lifestyle and the need to explore—there's something about *him*, the warlock, that rubs me wrong. "We should've been picked up by now. She said it'd be four days max…"

He trails off when the sound of glass shattering splinters the calm they'd falsely believed in, the loud crash reverberating against each wall on this floor. It's coming from another unit, much like this one, that we use for questioning. Of the two, this one is the most restrictive with only one exit.

For a few minutes after, both men look shaken, quiet and pensive, but then there's a shift in the older witch's expression. Anger now. His breathing is labored. "Are you sure we weren't screwed over by a pretty fae, Flavio? That *this* wasn't part of the plan?" It's a low hiss grit out from between clenched teeth while he runs a tired hand down his face. In a normal setting, he'd appear about forty, but the dirt and lack of proper nutrition are making him appear gaunt. *A weak warlock.* "When are we getting paid again? Have you seen any of the money promised?"

"Don't start, *Angelo*. The instructions were simple when you agreed." An exasperated sigh comes from who I now know as Flavio. His head tilts back then and he stares at the ceiling for a minute or two, almost leisurely, but then his head snaps down and he leans forward. Closer to his mate. "Don't pin this on me—you knew the risk involved, cousin, when you agreed, balls deep inside her warm cunt while I took her ass. No sense in panicking now. We need to find a way out unscathed and then find that saucy fae."

"How? They have us under lock and key."

"Do they?" Flavio raises his arms and smirks. Where they are now is more of an interrogation space, just a table and a few chairs inside and they're sitting opposite each other. No restraints. The doors aren't closed. "Seems we are free to go if we're careful about it."

Angelo's shaking his head, hands clenching atop the table. "It can't be that easy."

"Sometimes things in life are."

Since their capture, Flavio acted as the most drugged lunatic out of the two, someone completely outside of his faculties and consumed—afraid of his own shadow as if they were hallucinations until earlier today. That's when the game changed; my guards still believed them to be under some sort of unexplained influence when they caught him snorting a powdery substance.

The werewolf king was right: too many coincidences become intentional.

It wasn't a human drug they confiscated—we have no idea how they manage to conceal it under our noses either—but this drug isn't one I'm familiar with. Aware of. It's the color of dirt and smells of rotted fruit, yet when they brought the small bag containing the substance to me shortly after I'd hung up with Xadiel, I understood both him and Theodore like never before.

Both men miraculously are awake and aware after days of pretending, found talking before being moved, and now they sit opposite each other on metal chairs with a table between them made of the same material. It also reeks in there, the stench of fear hitting my nose while I pass the two guards on duty.

Both men came here willingly. Too complacent, and they were imbecilic to do so.

To talk freely where anyone could hear them. With today's technological advances, I could be watching and listening from anywhere.

"Fucking dumbass." They couldn't hear me when I was invisible, nor could they sense me. Flavio and Angelo had been in neighboring cells until a short while ago, sleeping side by side in rooms with bars instead of walls. No glass. Not much in the name of separation. Just like now, I've given them no reason to believe there's more to this than my concern.

Because the Wiccan king must take care of his people without question, and it's my honor to do so.

The healer from earlier found nothing outside of a substance in their system that would flush out naturally. Herbal, yes, with a touch of blood, which surprises me, but with nothing known to counteract the effects of what they took.

So I waited.

Rest. Sleep. To be kept locked away and safe until it passes.

Until now.

The little they ingested lasted all of thirty minutes to dilute in their system. No more excuses. They took my kindness for a fool, and now, I smile while striding past the two warriors stationed outside the entrance silently watching the floor. They cannot hear or scent anything being off until I place a hand over each man's shoulder and squeeze.

That was the signal of my arrival, and they heed it. Keeping up the pretense, they each give a subtle tilt of the head in a minute bow before regaining their rigid stance. Both stare straight ahead. Both smile just a tiny bit.

"We were paid to be a distraction—nothing else. If we're caught..." Angelo trails off, barely moving his lips so as to not draw attention while pushing his long hair back. "This is bad. I have a feeling—"

"That nothing in life is ever that easy, gentlemen." They both scream at the sound of my voice, nearly tripping over themselves to put space between us, but the cock of two guns as I seat myself at the edge of the table, stops them. Then there's the horrified look they each give me as I rematerialize, showing myself completely. I'm balancing the tip of my favorite dagger at the center of my palm, with no other weapon on me. None needed. "Or did you honestly think you'd get away with this farce?"

"Y-Your Majesty," Flavio stutters, then clears his throat a few times, swallowing hard. His face is ashen, but I'll give the moron credit for bowing his head in a false show of respect with what he thinks is a genuine smile. *He's as worthless as a piss stain.* "I...we... I don't have enough words to thank you and—"

"Is this the route we're going to take?"

"Of course, my king. We're so thankful and honored by your compassion."

"You truly are a piece of work, Flavio." That has him taking a step back; I just confirmed hearing everything they said. Up until this point, we didn't have a name or a way to identify these two. They'd been smart and carried nothing that'd give us any clue. "But I'll give you another chance. Are you ready?"

"I don't understand, my king." His perplexed expression is almost convincing, but the shifty eyes—he's unable to meet my eyes. Then there's the sweat beading on his brow while he shuffles from foot to foot, all unconscious movements but very telling.

"It's a simple yes or no question, warlock. I won't ask again."

"We are, King Leonardo. Our apologies," Angelo answers this time, but I don't take my eyes off Flavio. And the longer I stare, the more his body reacts and his fear permeates the air. It's heady in a different way, tantalizing but not sexually. No. This feeds that craving—the retribution my bloodline calls for as they're involved with the fae kingdom.

By love or because they fuck one; either way, they came with a deceitful purpose.

To take advantage of my kindness.

"Who sent you here?" One beat. Two beats. Nothing. So be it. The blade in my hand rips through the air before slicing across Angelo's cheek. It's a warning cut, shallow, and the few drops of blood currently running down his cheek are a punishment for playing games. "Is that too difficult of a question?"

"No." The older male's voice is low. Very subdued. "I'm sorry."

"Less apologies and more answers, warlock." My aura expands, and they feel the weight of each word. The command. "Who. Sent. You. Here?"

"We were paid to—"

"We were paid to try a healing mixture and had adverse effects, my king," Flavio says, effectively cutting his cousin off. He's smiling again, and the look is a bit creepy—obnoxious. "That's it. I swear it."

"Cut your bullshit. I already know." As soon as the last word leaves my lips, I disappear again and both men freak out. Their eyes are wide and their expressions frantic, turning from right to left in search of me before plastering themselves against the nearest wall.

Angelo is the smarter of the two, and he angles his body toward the still-open door before taking a sideways step. Then another.

He gets close enough to the exit that if he were to reach a hand out, it'd be just beyond the threshold. That's it. Not a single inch closer as alarm bells sound and metal doors slamming shut begin to pierce the air.

One by one, every door on this floor closes and then they're trapped inside with me while the guards outside the door walk away. They watch them do so through a small window at the center of the door. It's no bigger than the size of a large book and maybe an arm could fit through, something Flavio tests when he pushes Angelo aside and punches his hand through it, trying to get someone— anyone's—attention by waving his hand around like a lunatic.

"Please let us out! We're in here!" he screams while the other man's face drains of all color. The enormity of their stupidity is sinking in. Not slowly, but with the weight of a battering ram as a second later I'm lifting Flavio, dragging his arms roughly through the opening full of jagged glass and slicing open his arm. He cries out in pain and blubbers something about not being able to see me before I toss his body at the wall behind me.

There's a thud, the harsh sound of a hard impact before I scent blood in the air.

A coppery and tangy smell that has me craning my head from side to side. Not like Theodore would—I do not care to feed on this man—but because his pain brings me joy. If nothing else, I'll walk out of this room feeling lighter at another threat to my family—my people—being extinguished.

"Please, my king. Let's talk."

I'm standing before him before the man can take in another breath; I allow him to see me. "Then do so, Angelo. Answer my question, and all this ends here. You have my word."

"Don't, cousin." A cough. A groan of pain from his accomplice. "We can't."

"Is that your final answer?"

"Yes."

"N-no," they say in unison and I appear again, right in front of a pallid Angelo. He's shaking and his breathing is becoming choppy, the anxiety coursing through his body making it difficult for him to express himself. He starts and stops several times, no words coming out, but I'm a patient man and simply stand there. Watching him. Seeing how he breaks while behind me, there's a bit of noise, the groan of Flavio standing, and then my senses twitch the second I feel him touch my dagger. *Stupid move.* "King Leonardo, I'm sorry. We've made a grave mistake and—don't!"

I don't move. Don't dematerialize.

Instead, I chuckle. "Go ahead, Flavio. Just remember, I always pay back with kindness."

"And they'll make me a hero for this. There's a price on the head of every one of your family members." Instead of answering, I close my eyes and let him do as he must. This is me being benevolent; he will not kill me, much less with my weapon, and I'm proven right when the knife pierces my shoulder in a clean incision.

There's no pain. No burning sensation.

Rather, I'm given a taste of love with it as a beautiful pair of eyes appear before my closed ones. They're violet and a little large—an air of innocence in them that makes me smile—but what warms my chest and causes my cock to give a sharp throb is the slow flutter of her long lashes.

Who do they belong to? I do not know.

Yet something tells me they are real. This wondrous creature that's soothing the stab wound is important to me somehow.

"What have you done? You idiot!" Angelo screams, pulling me back to the present. It rends the air and hurts my ears a bit, but I breathe through the mounting need to smash his head in.

This warlock won't be killed today—there's usefulness in him—but I can't say the same for Flavio.

"I took care of their problem, cousin. King Larue wanted a diversion to take the woman and we outdid ourselves." Flavio's tone is cocky. Bold. Amused, yet it's his cousin I'm facing. Angelo sees my smile, the absolute fire in my eyes when I open them again, and he shakes his head while lowly pleading for mercy. The now dried blood on his cheek cracks with every word. *Please. I didn't want this.* He tries to gulp in air—choking on his desperation—while Flavio chuckles behind me, and I've yet to make a move. I'm calm, still under the effects of those gorgeous doe eyes as the blade is pushed in a little deeper. "Besides, Lilou promised me the free use of her lovely cunt and a lower fae female as a slave if I managed to kill a witch."

His own people. A confession heard by his king.

"Pray." One word, but it carries the promise of death. I'm not weakened in the least, and I don't remove the dagger from my skin. It's safe there for the time being. "I'll give you three minutes to do so."

I disappear again and move over to the opposite wall and directly behind the two. They're facing each other, their heartbeats increasing as the adrenaline rises—as fear takes over their nervous system.

One is shaking while he drops to his knees and bends forward until his head touches the cold, concrete floor. His words are muffled by the position, but I catch his pleas to the gods to help him. There's an apology or two mixed in, and I'm appeased by the way his crescendo grows until the cries of a scared man fill the room.

"Shut up!" Flavio hisses, his reaction different from that of his kin. He's sweating, yes, limbs shaking, and yet his bravado remains. The man swings in a circle, crazed eyes searching for that which he won't find until I decide, and yet he doesn't give up. "Help me find that knife. It couldn't have vanished with him."

That's where he's wrong; I can manipulate anything on my body. That includes weapons.

"Show yourself, Your *Highness*," a command, and I almost chuckle. Almost. The venom—how he spits out my title—earned him another strike against his already long list. "Be a man, and maybe I'll make your death one with dignity. I'll let *you* pray like your mother did before they killed her."

The wrong choice of words.

I know that. Angelo knows that.

Red: the color of violence and life, representing both sides of the spectrum, and my eyes see nothing but the hue as I strike. In the blink of their eyes, I'm behind him, leaving an inch or two between us as I manifest and kick the back of his knees. They buckle and his body weight crashes hard on the ground, a pained groan leaving his lips, but he has bigger things to worry about than bruised knees.

Unadulterated rage has taken hold of me, and I'm yanking the piece of shit's head back until there's an unnatural crack heard, the sound of a vertebra breaking under my force, but that's not what I need. I want his pain while my magic demands retribution.

To cleanse the floor with a crimson wash. To hear the screams of pain.

Nothing else but watching the life drain from his face will suffice or calm the warlock in me.

And for the first time, I'm not above my brothers-in-law—no sense of peace or rationale left in me as I yank the blood-stained opal dagger from my flesh and return the favor. I puncture the side of his neck, push it in deep as Flavio screams, and then slice him from one side of his neck to the other. The blade cuts through him as if he were butter, surgically opening him deep enough that I'm able to stick two fingers alongside the blade and press on his trachea.

He's frantic and trying to push my hands away, eyes wide and scared while his life's essence spurts. It coats my shirt and face, some of it landing on the back of Angelo's head who refuses to rise from his place on the ground.

"Would you like to pray now?" My tone is condescending, meant to taunt him. There's a gurgle as the blood accumulating chokes him. He's having a hard time breathing, and I give Flavio comfort by unleashing a bit of my power as his king upon him. And for as much as he wishes to fight against the aura, his body betrays him, and the neck with my fingers buried deep alongside my dagger bends for me, further creating damage.

Rivulets of red flow like an open faucet, creating a warm puddle beneath him. With each of his heartbeats, it grows and his chest labors, his clammy skin becoming more pallid by the second.

Bending a bit over him, I use my other hand to smack him just hard enough that his hazy eyes snap to mine. I have a minute of his attention at best, but it's enough for what I need to say.

"Your biggest mistake was coming onto my lands and mentioning my mother. I could've given you an easy death, taken mercy and shot you in the head once, but you were cocky." There's a fluttering beneath my fingers as if he's trying to answer me but can't. There's no swallowing or clearing of the throat that will help him, and the more he tries, the faster he'll die. I shake my head at him and press a little harder, enough to send a sharp jolt of pain and stop him. "Your words mean less than shit to me, warlock. My family is sacred, and you tried to rise against them; I will never forgive that. May Thanatos cross you into the afterlife and Hades condemn you to eternal suffering."

A presence is felt in the room now, ominous and dark, and Angelo looks up just in time to watch the haze of death cover his cousin. He freezes, a puddle of piss growing around him, while the God of Death is here and gone within seconds, leaving behind a corpse. A corpse whose chest is rising for a final time, the air having gotten trapped, but then it doesn't matter as I tear out the mangled piece of the windpipe and toss it at the paralyzed witch.

"You will tell me everything, Angelo."

"Yes, my king."

"Then start. I have a plane to catch in a few hours. Tell me who and where *she* is, asshole."

CHAPTER 6
Anaya

"*Anaya, go and welcome our guest. The Luna is awake.*"

Father's voice rings through my head, the sharp bite in his command causing a yelp to slip past my lips as the cup of water I'd been drinking crashes to the floor. It shatters upon impact, the shards nicking at my bare feet while a wave of nausea rolls through me.

"What the gods is this?" I hiss, placing one hand over my forehead while the other presses on my stomach, willing the horrid feeling to go away. For a few seconds, I feel no change—the urge to curl into myself almost causes me to drop to my knees—but I manage to stay upright. I walk away from the mess made and head toward the bathroom, one slow step at a time until I'm standing in front of the mirror.

The sight before me is ghastly. Not me.

I've always been fair-skinned, but this is more. This has nothing to do with the minimal amount of sunlight I've been allowed over the years, less since my mother's death, or the lack of nutrients I consume as my meals are made to keep me thin and weak.

No. This is dark magic, and the proof is found the second I concentrate on my aura. The cerulean blue, a gem-like tone with hints of purples and greens, is there but muted. Being constrained. There are shades of black, vine-like manacles restraining me while simultaneously draining me.

"How is that tea still affecting me? It's been days." I recognize the trails of magic, though. Its signature belongs to my father, yet at the end of the tight grip, there's a hint of Brice. *Is this how they planned to force my hand into marriage? Controlling my motor functions?* "Merde. Or did they do something else to me? Could it be the water?"

Anaya, did you not hear me? I said—

My apologies, my king. I was in the shower and I'm getting dressed now.

I know I'll pay for interrupting him, and I'm not surprised when a second later it feels as though someone's driven a rusty pike through my skull. It hurts, and this time it's worse than anything I've felt before. I can't stop myself from rushing to the toilet and losing the little bit of water I drank a few minutes prior; I'm gasping and choking, clutching my head while bile mixes and the acidic taste burns my throat.

It takes a few minutes for me to stop and regain my equilibrium, for the shaking to slow, but when it does, he's there again. Almost as if he waited for me to stop, knew the exact moment I did.

You have five minutes, Anaya. See that the Luna is taken care of and happy.

Yes, Father.

Crawling, I make it to the sink and use the countertop to pull myself up. I'm shaky, stomach still giving small heaves, but I push it back and open the faucet. The water here is cold, the heating taking a while to reach the desired temperature, and I call it to me once it's lukewarm.

I don't have the strength to wash my face, but at the quirk of a few fingers, the water dances for me and curves high enough to gently wash my face. It reaches my hairline and then glides over my closed eyes and the curve of each cheek, removing every trace of the tears I've shed before falling down the drain. This happens a few times, each sweeps soothing my frazzled nerves before there's a knock at the door.

No one enters my room, but the scent of a fae male hits me shortly after.

Another guard. Another of my father's faithful devotees.

"Princesse Anaya, I've been sent to escort you." His tone is monotone, with no emotion or inflection. And I don't answer him, choosing instead to take another minute and gather myself before deciding at the last minute to change my dress. The zipper at the side of this one runs from just below my breast to the hip and it falls to the floor after a show shimmy, pooling on the floor in its ridiculous yellow tone with lace overlay and pearl beads at the bust.

Not that the ones inside my closet are any better, but at the least, I can choose to greet the Luna in something a little more subdued. Sure, it's in the palest of greens and as conservative in length as the rest, but out of all the gowns delivered an hour after I woke up yesterday, this one was made for me by my mother before her passing.

The last one. A birthday gift the day I turned eighteen summers.

Father kept us dressed to his liking, but Mother always tried to make it special by designing them herself, and the one I'm holding now, I could never hate. Not when it was made with love.

Slowly, I slip it on, carefully avoiding the areas Brice burned with his possessive touch. Yet it still stings a bit when the fabric settles over the area, and the way he's watching me—his threat yesterday and the unafraid way he grabbed me—leaves me with little to no choice, and I heal myself slowly.

I do my best to neutralize the pain, but not erase it as my father pierces our connection once again.

Treat her like the queen she is. Understood, Daughter?

Yes, my king.

"Princesse? Are you ready?" the guard calls again, followed by a sharper knock. He's impatient now but doesn't say anything else when I exit the room a few minutes later. I'm used to being the perfect version of myself, and touching up my light makeup or making sure my hair is appropriate at all times is something I can do in my sleep. Robotically.

"This way, Princesse Anaya. Please follow me. Your father—"

"Has already relayed his instructions. Please lead the way."

"Of course." With a nod, the fae male turns and walks down the corridor outside my bedroom. His strides are faster than mine, forcing me to almost jog to keep up right before he turns left, and the dreariness of my sector crashes with the oppressing nature of the heavily armed guards gathered outside another door. This short hallway has no other exit outside of where we came from, and had I not seen this myself, I would've never believed the amount of military personnel watching the very space occupied by the wolfen Luna.

A sickening feeling grows, settling in my stomach the closer we get. Each footstep isn't quick enough, my powers demanding that I move, shield, and protect this woman I've never met before. And the closer I get, the stronger the magic flows, so much so that a man not far from me drops and kneels as my approach finally catches their attention.

Heads turn in my direction, and the audible shift of weapons is loud; they're each holding a high-caliber rifle with a translucent bullet full of a silver-ish liquid inside of an open-view magazine. One by one, they adjust them while watching me with furrowed brows. Confusion—overwhelmed by the need to submit—it's all there in their matching expressions.

They don't understand why they're reacting this way, but I ignore it while taking in two very slow and deep breaths. I let each out slowly, careful to not unleash any more of my tethers. Instead, I draw them back. Force my dominating essence into hiding and simultaneously, they take a collective breath of ease, more so the man who escorted me here from my room.

His posture becomes rigid seconds later. His eyes are a little too curious.

The questions are there. They all watch me with trepidation as the fae's military has always regarded me as nothing more than the daughter of the man they worship. I'm an accessory to be protected, but never listened to or worse, bowed to. Nothing more than a quiet and unimportant presence, unless I'm brought before the public and used to bring comfort to our people.

Because they trust me. Not all believe my father to be righteous or fair.

Moreover, they're unsure if it's me or the Wiccan princess confusing them.

Ignoring them, I move shakily toward a small table directly across from the slightly ajar door. There's a lamp sitting atop it and a tray with a carafe of water, the matching crystal glass sitting beside it with a plain white napkin over it.

My instinct is to serve the woman inside, to do what little I can and make her stay as comfortable as possible, but then I'm stopped in place. Voices drift. Angry ones, and instantly I'm furious.

"You cannot shoot her, Brice!" Lilou, Brice's sister, shouts then. *When did she get here? Why is she here?* As far as I knew, Lilou's been sent out of the kingdom on a mission by my father. Been absent for months now.

It's made my life a little easier, too.

Her dislike for me isn't hidden, while mine is contained behind a quiet dismissal, by ignoring her behavior when she throws a snide comment my way.

Sleeping with my father and brother has made the cheap fae woman brave. Stupid, too.

"You're right, but there are other ways to gift pain," Brice's voice booms, his rage thundering and reaching far outside the room they're occupying. Neither sibling is mumbling anymore or being discreet. Instead, each word is clear and the threat is concise. Each guard is attuned to it, too, not stepping in but choosing to listen.

Their pointy ears twitch while their heads tilt. They lift their weapons high, muzzles aimed at the door as if Brice and Lilou are under threat.

Not me. I rush toward the door, my hand on the handle, when the same guard that escorted me here places a hand on my arm.

"You shouldn't go in there yet. Brice and Miss Lilou—"

"Are forgetting who's in charge." I keep my tone even, hiding the bout of ire currently pulsing in my veins. And for as much as I try to keep playing the act of a sweet and soft princess, I can't fight back the bristling of my wings—how they manifest themselves as easily as a werewolf can shift. How the fangs of a vampire drop into place. Their luminescent-pearl-like shade darkens the longer this man touches me, something he picks up on and mumbles a low *sorry* before letting go. "Never do that again."

"Yes, Princesse."

"And two, *your* king's instructions were very clear. She's to be treated with respect."

"But she's a witch."

"Ask him yourself, then." That makes him blanch, while the others standing rigidly take a step back at the suggestion. They fear my father, a man who's never so much as picked up a sword outside of shows of dominance. He's a leader; his men do the fighting—die in the name of his cause—while the glory goes to him.

One day I'll get away. Maybe that's why—

"I'm going to make your life hell as payment for the life your mate took." Brice's threat pulls me from that thought. It's followed by this weird cracking sound, like a sharp spark, moments before the scent of something burning hits me.

"What in the goddess..." I push the door open before anyone can attempt to stop me again, rushing inside and gasping at the sight. The wolfen Luna is tied to a wall by metal shackles, her clothes dirty while Brice and his sister stand over her, each wearing a matching, disgusting grin.

In his hand, though, there's a weapon I've never seen before. A taser; I watch it discharge another bolt against her skin, the prongs digging deep.

You can tell she's in pain.

I see it. Feel it somehow.

How is this even happening?

Her eyes roll for a second, but then the Luna snaps herself out of it. She's shaking her head while biting the inside of her cheek, and yet, not a single sound of pain escapes her.

Her strength is admirable.

Her aura is pure.

Our eyes meet for a second before the sound of a low growl causes my head to snap toward the culprits. Lilou looks constipated, her favorite expression, while her brother, for some reason, is intrigued by my sudden appearance. From head to toe, Brice gives me a salacious once-over—stopping a second or two over my injured hips—and I shiver in repulsion. He notices and smiles, enjoying the way he makes me uncomfortable, something his sister rolls her eyes at while I place myself between them and the Luna.

"Who gave you permission to hurt her?" For the first time, I let them see my displeasure. It catches the two off guard just for a second, and had I not been so worried about the woman behind me, I'd find some amusement in it. "Answer me."

Brice is worried.

Lilou takes a step back, face pinched tight. She's not used to me pushing back, but something about the prisoner has me on edge. I've abandoned my vows to stay under the radar to keep her safe.

I can't be any other way. Something commands me to, and it's beyond me.

"Anaya, what are you doing here?" The taser is turned off immediately, his tone doing a complete one-eighty from the menacing hiss he spat at the chained Wiccan royalty. Falsely soft. Meant to demand my compliance in front of everyone within hearing range. "This is no place for our prin—"

"I'm beyond disappointed, General. You two fail at common decency," I cut him off, something that angers the siblings. One narrows his eyes while the other bares her teeth.

"Watch it!" Lilou snaps, moving toward me with her hand raised, but is stopped by Brice. His hand grips the back of her shirt, nearly ripping the side with his harsh tug. "Let me go! What are you doing, Brother?"

"Did King Larue send you, Anaya?"

"Yes." My answer deepens his frown, yet I'm focused on preparing myself for any incoming attack. I don't trust either of these two. "He had me escorted and doesn't want a single hair touched on this woman's head. His words."

"I see." Two words. Nothing else.

"That's it, Brice? You're just going to—"

"Silence."

The room grows silent outside of the slightly labored breathing from the witch. She's exhausted and hurt, but her magic is strong. I feel the ripple of her power as it encased the room and then removed a single bullet from a gun without drawing attention.

I've known about her and her sister all my life.

Born with gifts and a target on their backs. One controls death while the other dances with foresight, telling the future without the need for touch or proximity—Father fears them, but the telekinetic ability is something no one is aware of.

For a second, my head turns and our eyes meet, and I notice she's losing consciousness. Her head lolls and her body sags in her shackles, chaffing her skin while the blood on her lip continues to drip slowly onto her plain shirt. She nods at me, and I hear that voice again. Weaker than before.

Remain calm. He's coming.

"Look at me, Anaya. What did he send you here to do?"

It's hard to do so, but I look away and refocus on the duo in front of me. "I've already stated my purpose—"

"Why does he want her protected and cared for?" Brice's jaw ticks. Anger pulses from him in waves, yet I'm not afraid this time. For once, I feel a little sense of vindication because I'm not alone—for some unknown reason, this wolfen Luna and Wiccan royal has sparked an ember of hope in me. "What is he planning?"

"If you have a problem with that, ask him. King Larue enjoys being questioned."

CHAPTER 7
LEONARDO

I'm already there when the werewolf king's private jet touches down on the tarmac.

Xadiel and my sister exit first, followed immediately after by Theodore. They're talking to each other in low tones while their matching expressions mimic mine, a mixture of worry and anger, the latter of which being the most predominant. It ripples through the runway and their guards and mine feel it, all falling to one knee as the oppressive aura forces their submission.

No one complains, though. They understand and want the same result:

The fae king and his lineage dead.

Isabella home and standing beside her werewolf mate.

Once they reach the bottom of the plane's stairway, pleasantries are kept short with a simple handshake from both brothers-in-law while Gabriella wraps her arms around my midsection and cries softly. From anguish. From not spending much time with me since her rebirth.

"After we find Isa, my hundred-year-old promise to make you both eat a frog still stands." That breaks the tension a bit and she snorts, lightly punching my arm. My shirt is wet from where she's hidden her face, causing me to grimace. *Gross.* "Make that the biggest flying insect I can get my hands on. I still remember how you two shrieked if one landed on you."

You'd think with the connection we hold to nature that something like that wouldn't bother them, but I remember differently. When our parents died, they'd just been coming into adulthood while I was just thirteen summers, giving me plenty of time to be that annoying little brother who bugged them constantly when possible.

Not that my sisters complained. They gave as good as I dished.

If I pranked them, they stole my dessert.

If I made fun of them, they'd return the favor every time I failed to cast the simplest of spells.

"Shut it." It's hissed low with no real malice, but the ears of my twin sisters' mates perk up. A tiny bit of amusement comes from them —me—and the atmosphere eases enough that those kneeling slowly rise and retake their positions. Not that Gabriella notices; she's too busy jabbing her finger into the spot she'd previously hit. Punches me in the gut, too. "You snitch, and I'll bite you. Or worse…"

At her trailing off, I give her a bigger squeeze. Tighten my hold on her. "Temper, temper, dear sister. Has becoming a vampire made you prone to violence?"

"What's this he's talking about, pretty girl?" Theo and I speak at the same time, but at his nickname for her, Gabriella's rigid posture relaxes and a small chuckle slips through. "Are you afraid of something?"

Lifting her head from my chest, Gabby glares at me before turning her head toward her mate, the softest of looks given to him. "Never ask me that again, love."

"We'll talk about this after." He's looking at her, but the response is directed at me.

"Do so, Your Highness, and I'll make you pay."

"What are little brothers for, Gabby?" Shifting my gaze toward my vampire brother-in-law, I smirk. "After we bring Isabella home, I think it's time I sat down with both of you. The stories I have..."

"After," Xadiel interjects. He's not upset over our interaction; the man's used to my relationship with his mate—shares one with me as a true brother would—but I know he needs us to re-shift the focus. The book in my hand catches his attention, and I give him a nod. "That's one of the ancient scripts they were after that night, isn't it? What your uncle was searching for when the fae woman appeared and stabbed Silla before your sister and I arrived?"

Because you'll need it more than once.

This is what he meant that day. One time to save Gabriella, and the other for Isabella.

"Yes. I've kept it safe all these years as our father instructed. He knew."

"When was this?" Gabriella completely steps out of my embrace now and after tugging my shirt so I can bend down to her level, she gives my cheek an affectionate kiss. That's the end of the small talk as all amusement dies and the attention turns toward our father's book. She takes it from me and I let her, her pale fingers skimming down the leather-bound front, her longing for our parents felt through our familial bond. "It's been so long since I've seen this. Since I've been home to our people and—"

"We have time." Tears pool in her eyes, but they don't fall. Her hybrid nature won't allow them to, but I get it. There's so much to say and people who miss her. "But first, we need Isa home for that reunion. Let's find the stubborn seer."

WE'VE BEEN HOLED up in the alpha's home for a few days now, going through everything Isabella left behind to point us in the right direction. She's a cryptic one, but concise, and I know that with her, the timing is never off. We are meant to know the next move when it's time and not a second before.

Her sacrifice won't be in vain, even if it makes me want to throttle her.

Since we were young, she's carried the weight of the world on her shoulders, always taking on the role of protector and guide. Being a seer shaped that narrative, more so when it comes to us, her family. Our pain is unacceptable to her, but what she fails to realize is we feel the same.

Her hurt is ours. Our bond as siblings allows it to be no other way.

"Do you think Silla is with her?" Gabriella asks while her mate flips through Isa's notes, trying to find something we might've missed. He left yesterday for Seattle and came back today with the Stygian blade, the same one Isabella explained needs to be delivered to the underworld. "That she's involved?"

"To be honest, I don't know." A truth I've had no choice but to confront. Signs point to this not being a coincidence, the wording in Larue's threat being one of them. The limited knowledge my prisoner back home had wasn't much to go on, but he did confirm that a powerful witch needed escorting home. "Right now, it can go either way."

"Talk," I say, grabbing one of the chairs they'd been using and turning it around. I'm seated in his direct line of sight after kicking over the still-bleeding-out body of his kin. Flavio's body is still warm. "I'm listening."

Angelo wets his lips and swallows hard, pleading with his eyes for me to give him a second or two to compose himself, which I grant. A nod is all I give, but he understands and wipes a hand down his face, wincing a bit as it catches the crusted blood and tugs it off, reopening the natural seal the sanguine drops created. "I'm sorry."

"I'm sure you believe you are." Not going to sugarcoat it for him. He came here of his own free will and agreed to whatever plan they'd concocted. This remorse comes from getting caught and nothing else.

"It was never supposed to end this way. Just a clean job." He exhales roughly as tears form in his eyes, but I'm not moved. I'm annoyed.

"You will not get sympathy from me. Get to the point before I lose my last strand of patience." It was a command from his king, one enforced by the magic we're bound by. Its effect is instantaneous; he bows his head while his lips begin to move.

"Flavio knew the full details. I was asked to accompany him and help, that we were here so a scared witch could have safe passage home. That she was strong—special—but would not leave otherwise and we'd be saving lives."

"That's it? You walked in blind otherwise?"

"Yes, Your Highness." Angelo's tears fall then, his stare full of anguish as it moves over to his cousin. "That's what he and the fae woman led me to believe. I was stupid, know better, but I'd been under the influence of sex and mushrooms at the time—I believed it was an easy job with good perks. I'd get another taste of her cunt and more money than I've ever seen."

"Who financed this? Paid the two of you."

"King Larue."

"An enemy to my crown." Not a question, and his entire body once again bends toward the ground. Head pressed to it. "I want the woman's name, Angelo. Who is she?"

"Flavio introduced her as Brice's sister, but no direct name."

"So you do have some doubts?"

I nod, rubbing the short beard on my face. Haven't shaved in days. "More than one, to be honest, but I can't focus on that right now. Nor why the name Brice infuriates me the way it does."

I know no man with that name.

At that, Gabby looks up from her position over the map with a raised, sharp brow. "I detect jealousy in your tone, Brother."

Ignoring her jab, I push all thoughts of what my prisoner said to the back of my mind for now. The focus here is Isabella and Silla, and so far the information the old warlock gave was useless, something everyone in this room concurs with.

I'd told them of the deception after our greeting out on the tarmac and they agreed that I'd keep Angelo alive for now. He still may be of some use, at the least to identify the female and whoever *Brice* is.

"Isa didn't mention Silla, but that doesn't mean anything. The timing is just too convenient."

She knows I'm deflecting and narrows her eyes. "Our sister didn't mention anyone, and you know the why, Leo."

"Because she's stubborn?" At that comment, Gabby snorts and rolls her eyes before reaching over for a monogrammed pen with the alpha king's name on it. It's in the colors of his crest; dark green with gold lettering that stands out. He's given us free use of anything inside his home and on these lands but is choosing to remain outdoors.

Between him and Tero, they're combing the area in search of a grimoire belonging to our father.

Another piece of the puzzle she'll reveal when it's time.

"We both know Isa will never reveal anything until it's the right time. She's selfless and reckless and—

I blocked your gift once.
I move in ways you'll never predict, and my close ties
know how to block your sun.

Those words slam into me then for some reason, pushing all noise away, and while I see Gabriella's lips moving, I can't make out a word. Instead, I'm reminded of a story my aunt used to tell me as a child. A fable about a girl considered to be an abomination; the daughter of an exiled warlock and a dark magic fae that was hated by both of her kind.

They didn't trust her.

Called her the enemy hidden in plain sight. Strong enough to destroy what feeds the earth—our days and nights.

And while Larue's threat isn't exact, the similarities are too glaring to ignore. Just like I know Silla's hidden the true extent of her abilities from us, choosing to practice light magic—spells to aid those who are sick or to help our gardens flourish. It's why I've never doubted her, but I can't help but think about her story now in connection to the letter the fae king left my sister.

One part, to be exact:

> *She was a child who danced a fine line between the light and darkness that haunted humanity, a witch fairy with dangerous aspirations. To block the gifts given by the gods, one must destroy the sun before killing the moon.*
>
> *Only then will she be free.*
>
> *Reign over those who hurt her.*

"What do you say? Don't know, or you hope?" Gabriella's voice cuts through whatever fog I'd been under then, effectively bringing me to the present. Out of that memory. Away from the many times our aunt shared the same story that right now feels like a forewarning.

Is that what she's been doing all these years? Preparing me?

But why? To what gain?

"A little of both." The opal dagger Xadiel gifted me glints at that moment, having caught a ray of sunlight, and that catches all of our attention. Since our arrival, there's been an overcast gloominess surrounding the forest that matches our emotions, yet a single ray peaks through the clouds now and that same pull I felt over a century ago when this blade first touched my hand beckons me.

A low hum, a vibration that brings forth a sense of comfort I don't quite understand.

My chest settles and falls into a rhythm with the pulse, causing the room and people inside to become nothing but a dull shadow in the background as I reach over and pick it up. It's warm in my palm and heavy; I close my hand around the hilt and tighten my grip while taking in three very deep breaths.

And it's on that third exhale that I see. As if a veil has been removed, and I don't fight the way I'm being shown every single aspect that before made no sense, but now looks like a separate map.

From the books that are spread all across the Luna and Alpha's desks inside their joint office, each one being used to decipher or scribe for our sister. Because everything we touch carries a hint of our essence, and hers is all over this room—home.

I can see the literal trace of her presence now. Her magic.

Evidence of the life she's built with her husband, a man who's slowly losing control of his beast, surrounds us. He's angry, understandably so, and being ridden hard by the animal he shares a body with. The wolf wants its mate back. It doesn't understand anything outside of his need for her, and the pain-filled howls it unleashes every night only fuel our need to bring her home.

Just like now, outside these walls, there's the angry growl of an alpha wolf. It reverberates throughout the land and the cadence shakes this room; it sweeps across every place his queen has touched.

Merges with her magic and highlights what we didn't see at first.

How is this happening?

I know the other two are talking and that questions are being asked, but I'm too focused on balancing the tip of the dagger on my finger while following the vibrant lines. Like a maze, yet they all end by a globe of the earth.

One that's showing me the North American continent, but more specifically, the trace highlights Canada. The area of Quebec.

A smile spreads across my face and everything shifts back into focus, erasing the magic trails I'd been following.

Thank you, Goddess.

"What's going on, Leo?" My head turns toward my sister. She's watching me curiously, her expression hopeful. "Why are you smiling like—"

"I found something, pretty girl," Theodore speaks up, causing our heads to snap in his direction. He's holding up the note Isa left for Xadiel to find, his red eyes blazing with fury. The vampire king's taken this more than personally; he feels guilty. Holds regret. "We've just been too blind to see it."

"What do you mean, Theo?" Gabriella stands from her place behind Isa's desk and steps beside her mate. As their skin touches, the smallest bump of the arms, a haze of bright red surrounds them, and it's strong. A united heart. "Show me."

"Look at the bottom right-hand corner and tell me what you see?"

"There's nothing…" my sister trails off, but then tilts her head. She's squinting a bit, the red of her irises brightening as a smile stretches across her lips. "Those are coordinates. Isabella left us a way to find her."

"That's Quebec."

"She's in Canada," Theo and I say in unison, both raising a brow at the other. My brother-in-law is a man of few words unless it's toward his mate. I get it. Don't have a problem with it, nor am I intimidated by the vampire king. It's why I merely give him a shrug and turn my attention back to Gabriella; she's watching us with a perplexed expression. "She left multiple clues."

"Where? We've been combing this place for days."

"This globe, for one." No sooner do the words leave my lips than the dagger balancing on my finger embeds itself in the same place I'd seen earlier. I didn't throw it. No one moves for a few seconds after, either, but that all changes as another angry growl rips through these lands.

The coordinates and where my blade lands are the same. Tero enters the room in his snake form, and he's holding a grimoire I recognize and accept from him.

No other words are exchanged. None are needed as we move through Xadiel's house, and all going in different directions. I'm heading toward her hemlock tree for a secondary look around while Theo and Gabriella say goodbye. He has a visit to make and the God of Death awaits his son, while Gabriella will give the alpha wolf some reprieve.

He'll have his mate back soon.

Yet something tells me there's more to this. And it's confirmed as I stand in front of Isabella's altar and the color of amethyst blankets over the space like a comforting haze.

It gave me the same sensations the blade does—as if I'm tied to it.

As if it's *mine*.

CHAPTER 8
Anaya

"Hello, little mate."

I'm frozen in place by those three little words—the last thirty minutes. In the span of a few days, I've had my world thrown upside down, once again seeing the cruelty in my father's eyes, but nothing could have prepared me for the complete devastation those three words have caused.

Hello, little mate.

I can't put into words the feelings coursing through me. Everything feels like too much.

From the noise, to my skin, to my emotions; I'm a mess and can only freeze in place and try to gather what's left of my faculties.

There's confusion, loss, and hope...

The latter of which Isabella introduced me to and is the most dangerous. Since meeting her, there's been a small kernel growing within me—taking root deep inside my chest while I've embraced her as a part of me. As I plan a way to save her; I'd sacrifice myself if need be.

Getting to know Isabella, taking care of her—not because my father demanded it, but because I have to. It's a need, this compulsion I can't nor will I question. We're tied in a way I don't understand, but I know this...

She's important.

To me. To so many, but this is more than I could've ever expected.

I should've asked instead of blindly trusting the words she mentally whispered to me since our first encounter. To not fear. That a *he* was coming.

All this time, I never questioned how our connection was possible. How we communicated without words, and sometimes a look was all we needed—a seer always knows and that's what I leaned on, but this is overwhelming. More than I know what to do with.

As is the possessive way this handsome man stares at me, cataloging my every breath. The most minute shift in my breathing and the perspiration dotting my forehead and the back of my neck. His nostrils flare, and without looking away he licks his bottom lip, and it's like a thunderbolt of need crashes into me, so much so that my knees weaken.

It takes everything in me to stay standing. To not move closer.

Because I know who he is. Introductions aren't necessary when Isabella's been my saving grace over the last few days and the familial similarities are striking. All three Moore siblings share traits —an aura of power and a cheeky grin that pulls at the corner of my lips.

It's been that way since the day I met Isa. Every time I've been in her presence and embraced her pure affection, this feeling of belonging would fill my chest and erase the misery my kin beat into me.

Will he blame me, though? Will her brother ever accept the daughter of his enemy?

No. I can't entertain this.

Isabella would've warned me. We've spent time a lot of time together and talked for hours on end while I brought her food or stayed close by in order to help her avoid being alone with any male. My brother and father are the ones I worried the most about. They had plans for her—wanted to break her—but then her mate came.

They all did, and thank the Goddess for that. She's going into heat soon yet remained calm, and I should've known her demeanor meant he was coming.

I don't think she meant her werewolf, though.

"I'm going insane. That's it," I mutter low and the warlock raises a brow. A sexy, amused grin curls at his lips, but he chooses to not answer. Instead, he lets me process everything…

In the last few days, I've been threatened and hurt.

I've been drugged and taken from my home country and to this cold and isolated building.

I put myself in the wrathful way of a man and his sister who want to destroy me.

Watched the God of War decapitate my father. Stood by as his blood bathed the floor inside this safe room while my brother tried to grab me and escape, but to me, these mini movie reels of time are nothing but distant memories. Nothing exists outside of this man's proximity and the scent of chocolate with complimentary notes of cloves infiltrating my senses.

It reminds me of cold winters and the comfort and warmth a decadent cup of hot chocolate brings. Thick, rich, and delicious. A hint of spice seamlessly envelopes the sweet; they merge and play—

tease me—and I find myself leaning a little forward before pulling back.

I smelled this before. Know I have.

Then I remember where: my mother's garden in that dream. His eyes are the same, too.

As is the warmth that seeps into my skin with his nearness. A few inches separate us, but to me, it's as if we are flesh on flesh.

And he's silently watching me while I take him in. Quiet and unconcerned with the craziness around us; a soft look slips onto his face that causes goosebumps to rise across my flesh. For a shiver to run down my spine while my nipples bead and push against the tight fabric of my dress.

A groan to the right of us is loud yet muted, but nothing takes precedence over his words.

They play on repeat.

Hello, little mate.

They grow louder in my ears while his tone deepens into a near growl.

Hello, little mate.

"What's happening to me?" No answer. No help. No explanation as to why I'm so entranced when fae soldiers lay dead on the ground. When my brother and forced intended are kneeling—the pain-filled sound coming from one of the two almost makes me look over, but then the man before me shakes his head, and I swallow hard. Even if I'm curious about the state of my kin, I don't dare look over.

I feel no guilt or hurt over what's happened here, and whatever the future holds for Ruben and Brice, it's karma's response to years of abuse dealt by these two men. But for once, I want to stand before them while they kneel, outnumbered. While I showed them they didn't break me.

"What's your name, little mate? Bless me with your voice." The timbre of his voice wraps around me in an invisible hug, tight and firm, while his eyes darken a bit. The beautiful blue takes on deeper tones while the pupil expands until there's nothing but a ring surrounded by endless black.

To anyone else, it would be frightening. To me, it's beautiful.

He holds my sole attention.

Your mate is dead, Anaya. He's using you.

The hurtful reminder comes from a voice inside my head, and I turn toward my brother. He's never spoken to me through our link, finds me useless and beneath him, and this is more proof of that. As if I will ever forget the pain I lived through and survived, leaving behind a hollow shell of the cheerful girl I used to be.

Father told me my mate was a fae of lower ranking who passed away, and while I've always suspected he was involved in the death, I've never doubted him. Not when I suffered through the torture of our bond breaking—wore the bruises marking my loss for weeks—before it all suddenly disappeared without a single physical trace left behind.

His explanation has also never changed. Not then, or at the dinner I recently interrupted in hopes King Larue would choose his daughter's happiness just once over his greed. To consider me as more than a commodity, versus a pawn he can move at his discretion.

It didn't surprise me that he let me down.

My pain meant little to a man who caused the death of his own mate. Because I lived through hell; my soul was ripped—torn in two —as the place where my mate would one day reside was stripped from me. Those agonizing days weren't a figment of my imagination.

I begged to end it all. To be put out of my misery.

Is he my second-chance mate? Or just another man coming to use me?

How could this tall man with reddish hair and a sharp jawline be mine?

How could this warlock accept me after everything my family has done?

"My mate is dead. You can't be him." The words leave me in a whisper but I know he heard it, and the deep rumble that comes from within his chest tugs at mine. It pulls my attention back to him, and it's instinctual how I raise my hand and rub at the spot, almost willing the throbbing organ to give me a reprieve while focusing on his azure eyes. How I raise a hand to touch him before catching myself at the very last minute. "This is a lie. Please stop."

"My princess. My mate." So much conviction in his roughened tone as it sweeps across my every nerve ending, lighting me up from within. The simple declaration fills every empty, bruised part of my soul with warmth. With peace. Something I've longed for—to no longer feel alone—but this can't be right.

Hope is a traitorous bitch, and I refuse to be hurt again. Can't afford to lose myself when freedom is within my grasp.

"Please don't lie to me. My mate is dead."

"I'm right here, little one." He takes another step closer and this time brings two large hands toward my face, cupping a cheek in each warm palm. His touch slams me right back to the memory of my dream, to the moment the shadowed figure touched my face and those piercing, blue eyes connected with my soul. I whimper. Can't bite back the sound because this is the real meaning of pleasure. Pure and raw, even if I don't want to believe it. "I'm alive and breathing and irrevocably tied to you until my last dying breath, and even then, I'll still be yours."

"It's a lie." I'm at a loss. Confused and hurt when Ruben tries to spew his demands once again. *Don't be naïve, Anaya. You're just easy pussy for him. The perfect revenge.* Those words, his nastiness pull an angry growl from me. It's nowhere near as menacing as the one a wolf or vampire would unleash, but Ruben and Brice are taken aback by it. It's there in their expressions and the way they lean back, more so when the man claiming to be my mate unleashes one of his own, and it's loud. Angry.

"What upset you, mate? I'll deal with it."

"My apologies, I—"

"I never want to hear those words come from your lips again."

He seems even angrier, truly upset by two words that to me are as natural as breathing—an instinct. But crazier than that is the way I touch his arm without conscious thought, placing my much smaller hand right over his bicep and watch the instantaneous change in his demeanor.

His chest ceases to rise and fall rapidly. His stance relaxes.

The snarl curling at the corner of his lips stops, turning instead into a cheeky grin, exposing the dimple on his right cheek. Highlighting the sharpness of his jaw and how handsome the small reddish beard there is.

I'm in trouble.

Get away from him, ma princesse. Don't make me hurt you!

You cheap slut. How can you touch the enemy? They killed our father.

The attacks come from both sides in unison, Brice and my brother forcing themselves into my head. They lash at my senses, the connection causing me to stagger and grab my head, whimpering as pain radiates across my skull. "Get out of my head!"

"Repay their kindness," I hear the warlock snarl seconds before his hands grip my hips so I don't fall. His touch sears me through the layers of clothing separating us, but I feel him, and it's complete bliss when I'm tucked against his chest. He's so much taller than I am, so much stronger, but it's home. There's no denying that. How he soothes me and his touch forces out their voices until there's nothing.

Not so much as a whisper.

Then, there's the electrical pulses that pass between us wherever we touch.

Different yet so delightful. Just what I need after the horrors of today.

One hand travels from my hip to the back of my head where he strokes his thumb up and down the length of my neck. He's much taller than me, and it shows when we're this close, his lips pressing against the crown of my head and even then, he has to bend a little to do so.

His breath sweeps across my hair, causing a few to move near my forehead. The warlock kisses that area, too. "Are you okay? Who hurt you?"

"My brother—"

"Knock him out, and ready both men for transport home." The gentle tone he'd used on me is gone, and who speaks is the king of Wiccans. Commanding—tinged with a bit of anger—and the guards who accompanied the three kingdoms present move into action. The ones already standing over Brice and Ruben are first to grab each man, hauling them up onto their feet.

They're forced to face us, and I feel their hateful stares. How they try to mentally attack me again, but at the first flinch, I'm released and pushed behind the king.

It happens so quickly.

I don't think and react.

The warlock walks over to them, hand striking out to grip Ruben's neck and squeezing it. My brother splutters and tries to move back, to shift and thrash as his hands are bound behind his back, but that seems to amuse the Wiccan king.

"You dare to hurt my mate?" Low. Vicious. A growl that affects me as much as my sibling and for opposing reasons. Prince Ruben is scared, while I'm given a shock to the system, and it's pleasant. Lovely. Thrilling in the way it sends a shiver down my spine, and the place between my thighs grows sensitive.

I'm wet. Positively dripping from the action.

This has never happened to me before. I'm a virgin. Completely untouched in every way.

"She's not yours. I'd kill her before she—" The single punch thrown by the man claiming to be mine knocks my brother off his feet and leaves him sprawled on the floor, unconscious. Just one hit, and there's a tear across the bridge of Ruben's nose and the top of his lip.

Yet that's not what I'm shocked by.

What causes me to break a rule that's assured my survival all these years is the blood dripping down the warlock's split knuckles. It's not a huge cut by any means, but the sight shakes me to the core.

I'm brought to tears and moving without thinking twice. I grab his hand and bring it to my face, kissing the laceration before closing my eyes and healing him. Within seconds, it's closed and his skin unmarred, but the silence that follows is haunting. Scares the hell out of me.

What did I just do?

"You've been holding out on us, ma princesse. That's going to cost you."

CHAPTER 9
Anaya

The threat in Brice's words causes me to take a step back and drop the warlock's hand—an action he doesn't like—and before I can put another few inches between us, I'm hauled against his chest with his nose skimming my hairline. No kiss this time, but instead, he breathes me in and whispers *strawberries and decadent cream* against my skin.

A simple act that brings so much pleasure, goosebumps rising everywhere. I can't deny his effect on me. Nor can I lie and say that the tingles my mother spoke about aren't there, how only your true fated mate can arouse you like this. And I am. My body doesn't feel mine, and the longer he holds me and his scent infiltrates my senses —embeds itself into my flesh—it's getting harder to deny him.

This.

Which leads me to one conclusion.

"He lied." It's muffled against his chest, my nose pressed tight to his torso. Then, there's the way the fae part of me vibrates with excitement. Because while we don't shift, our wings react and our ears twitch. They heat and pulse. And right now, both of these are sensitive.

More so my wings, and while folded at the moment—hidden within the span of my back—they tremble with need beneath my skin.

For his touch. For his admiration.

They're a part of what makes me who I am, and just like the rest of my body, they crave his attention. Just as a wolf would want their mate to pet its fur or a vampire wishes to have its fang licked, I desire this from him.

No man or woman has ever elicited this kind of reaction from me. Only my fated beloved, the other half of my soul can, solidifying the realization taking hold.

He's my mate. Mine.

"He truly lied."

"Who lied, precious one?" The arm wrapped around my back loosens its tight hold and I whine, a sound that's never come from me. It shocks me and I'm blushing, the heat on my face causing me to burrow deeper, which pulls a throaty chuckle from him. "Tell me, Miss…"

At his trail off, I snort. "Not that smooth, Your Highness."

"Your name, mate. I need it."

"It's Anaya."

"Anaya." The way he says it should be criminal. It's sensual and a bit enthralling, but at the same time settles the part of me that's lived under nervous duress for years. Isabella gave me a taste of this the moment we met, but never on this level. I go lax in his hold, no other way to explain it. "I'm King Leonardo to the world, my mate…" his voice is low so only I hear "…but to you, I'm just a man. I'm your equal. Simply yours."

"Mine." A whisper as a smile tugs at my lips. As my heart pitter patters. "Just mine."

"Yes. Always."

"Thank you." Because Leonardo's so tall, I don't attempt to kiss his cheek or chin—his lips—in public, but I do press my lips to his chest. Chaste. Yet the rumble that flows through him at the act gives me the confidence to do it again before hugging him once more and turning my head.

Because of how we're standing, I have a clear view of the rest of the room. Those alive stand nearby but give us some semblance of privacy. They've pulled a passed-out Ruben and a glowering Brice away, a few feet separating us now, but I barely give them a glance before meeting the set of eyes I seek.

She's glowing, a heated flush on her face while standing close to her mate, but Isabella is lucid enough to give me a nod. To mouth the words, *I told you.*

"Thank you," I mouth back in a whisper, but they're moving again. Her mate picks her up and nuzzles her neck; he's whispering to her, and I smile at the sight. I'm happy for her.

"Who are you thanking, precious?"

"Your—"

"Enough of this shit. That fae female is my bride-to-be." Brice cuts me off, and I'm physically repulsed by the reminder of what my father tried to do. I feel no pity as his corpse lies across the room, nearly cut in half by Aries's sword. Just like I feel no worry over the future that awaits his son and favorite guard. "Get your disgusting Wiccan hands off her. She's mine. Given to me by her father."

"No. She isn't." Lifting his unoccupied hand, the warlock traces a finger across my cheek and then taps the end of my nose. "This woman was always meant for a king, not a pauper."

"Tell him, Anaya. Tell him you're mine."

My reaction? I laugh. Maybe it's the nerves. Maybe it's the craziness of finding this man and my starting to believe his claim on me, but that's all that comes out.

This is what this male does to me. He makes me act out of character; I become unaware of my surroundings—unafraid of being punished.

Is this what being free feels like?

"That's as good an answer as I've ever heard. Don't you think?" Cocky, yet the ripple of anger that runs through the warlock holding me tight causes me to pull my head back. Just enough that I can meet Leonardo's eyes, and when I do, his soften immediately. "But I'll humor you, anyway." He's talking to Brice, but those smoldering eyes don't leave me. "Are you his fiancée, Miss Anaya?"

"No. Not by choice." No doubt. Complete honesty.

Leonardo's jaw ticks, but he nods. "Did Larue promise you to him?"

"Yes." My voice bares my shame, and after a second, I look away.

"Don't." The hand wrapped around my waist skims up my spine until it cups the back of my neck. His fingers expand and flex before tightening just a bit, enough to tip my face in his direction until our eyes meet again, violet on clear blue. "Much better."

"I never wanted to marry him. I begged my father to end it—"

"Relax. I'm not upset with you, Anaya." Another rush of pleasure at the way he says my name. Goosebumps rise and my breath catches, eliciting a warm hum from Leonardo. "You're innocent in this."

"How do you know that?" Tears form at the thought of him abhorring me for the crimes my father committed. Because of what he stole from all three of the Moore children. I've grown up with those stories; the lies and stolen glory King Larue sang about himself to anyone who would applaud him. Those blind followers who praised the man as if he were a god. "How do I know you truly don't hate me underneath it all?"

"Because I could never live without my heart."

"But Larue—"

"Is dead, and you're safe." Four words, and whatever bit of hesitation was left in me melts away. I initiate the hug this time, so tight and thankful. "I've got you, sweetheart. You don't have to do anything you don't want to ever again. They have no hold on you."

"Our fae princess will never be yours, warlock."

"She already is." Thunderous, the declaration reverberates throughout the room leaving no room for arguing. "This was deemed by the gods, and the only reason you're still alive is because I've allowed it. Because I want you to witness the acceptance of our bond. Show you what you'll never have."

"Thank you." Taking in a deep breath, I let it out slowly while giving him one more squeeze. This one's for me. To show him that while I have so much to still wrap my head around—conflicting voices and false narratives to swim through—I don't regret meeting him. Sure, I'll need a minute or thirty to catch up and truly embrace the newfound freedom he's offering, but I'm not going anywhere.

We'll figure this out together.

The moment he called me his mate has forever changed the course of my life.

I no longer wish to disappear and live alone for the rest of my existence, away from the fae realm or other societies. Maybe, just maybe, there's room for me in his, and slowly, I can learn that not everyone in my life is an enemy in disguise.

Leonardo can teach me to trust again. Show me what love is.

"Are you okay, precious one?"

With a small smile, I unwrap my arms from around him and then step out of his embrace. With a little distance between us, I let him see me. I don't hide myself or look down or tame my powers. This is me. "Do you promise to always be honest with me?"

"Yes." No hesitation. A bit of pride in his azure orbs.

"Do you think someday you can fully trust me?"

"Yes. Of that, I have no doubt."

"Do you have a sweet tooth? Because I haven't had a good piece of cake since my fifth birthday."

A sad expression overtakes his features at that, but he still gifts me a genuine smile. "I'll indulge that addiction every day for the rest of our lives. As your mate, that's my duty."

"That's all I need for now." What more could I ask for? We don't know each other yet, but it's a start. "But now, I need one more thing from you. I'm going to ask you to trust me."

"What are you...?"

"I'll be back." Without giving him a chance to finish his question, I turn and walk over to where Brice stands. He's a tall fae. Brawny and pompous, the latter of which comes across when he smirks at my nearness, yet before he can say a word, I turn my attention to one of the men holding him. "Sir, what's your name?"

"Augusto, Miss Anaya." He looks behind me at Leonardo before giving me a small bow. The soldier beside him does the same, and my guess is they're part of the Wiccan military. They wear similar colors, something I've noticed from each kingdom: they represent the colors or a pendant identifying their kingdom.

Wiccan. Wolf. Vampire.

"Augusto, can you please help the general in your custody down to his knees?"

As if sensing where this is going, a grin tugs at his lips and he nods. "Of course, ma'am."

"I've never had anyone 'ma'am' me before. It's a little weird." A few people chuckle, and I feel the most amusement come from Leonardo, his bond with me growing the longer we're in each other's presence. It's there, just small. Bigger than a kernel, more like a full pebble, and that hope his sister helped nurture clings to it, too. It gives me a reason to believe.

Gods, help me do the right thing. Guide me.

Brice's knees hit the floor hard a second later, the force sounding painful, but he merely glares at me. Sneers as I take the few remaining steps between us and inhale deeply, that foul stench turning my stomach, and I can't keep the grimace off my face. "I'd never marry you. Not before. Not ever."

"You have no choice."

"I do, and it would never be you. I loathe you."

"And you're a traitor." He spits and it lands near my feet; I'm disgusted by this but let him continue talking. This is the last time I'll ever be in his presence—I have my piece to say, too. "You let your people die and all because of a mate bond that will never save you. Your father and my sister didn't die in vain, Anaya."

"You don't care about your sister, Brice." The bullet Isabella pierced into Lilou's skull is still embedded into the floor beside her body. Her brain matter stains the ground, yet he hasn't shed a single tear. Hasn't shown an emotion other than anger over me. "You're mad that you lost. This is it."

"I'll have you."

"Brice, your scent repulses me. *You* sicken me." Reaching beneath the neckline of my dress, I take hold of the necklace he'd forced around my neck and give one hard tug. The chain pops, and I toss the remnants and ring against his chest. It bounces and rolls a bit away from his body but I feel no remorse—I'm lighter now. Can breathe better. "I will never be yours, not by force or choice."

"You'll pay for those words, ma princesse. This I vow."

"No. I won't." Then I do something else I've wanted to do for years. Rebel. Fight back. Closing my eyes to savor the moment, I pull my leg back and then kick him between his legs with every bit of the strength I possess. It isn't much as I'm not at a hundred percent, but the way he screams right after my heeled shoe connects with his testicles will forever bring me happiness. "May I never see you again."

"I'll kill him before he ever has a chance to, my female." Leonardo's warm body presses into my back, giving me someone to lean on. "Get him and the other fucker back home to Italy, Augusto. We'll be joining you soon."

"As you wish, Your Highness."

"We?" I ask while his men do as asked; I like the idea of going with him. Of spending time together, even if I'm unsure of everything else. With the king of faes dead and my brother arrested, I'm all the monarch has left. *They'd never accept a woman, though.* More than likely, the elders will step in and create problems for me in the royal court.

But how will the others feel? Those afraid and living under the dictatorship my father established, taking from those who have little to fatten his already full pockets? He's hurt more people than just this family or their mates; my fae kind is broken.

Our system is unjust. Cruel to those without a voice.

Maybe Leonardo can help, though? Fight with me to right these wrongs.

"Yes. We." Bending his head, he nuzzles my neck before giving the area a small bite. "I'm not letting you out of my sight."

"Good."

Suddenly, Isabella's voice breaks the bubble we've been under while they've talked or dealt with what happened here today. Our heads turn in her direction, and we find her clinging to Xadiel. Her heat is starting to hit her full force, and still, Isa places a hand on the doorframe to keep her werewolf from taking her past the threshold.

She's burrowing her head in his neck, but when she speaks, we hear her. "Somewhere in this building is Uncle Roberto. He never betrayed us." A deep breath in and a low purr begins in her chest, a call to her mate, and the hold he has on her body tightens. We see the way his black-tipped claws dig into her flesh where he holds her. "Silla was Larue's half-sister. He confessed this minutes before the first explosion."

Behind me, Leonardo stiffens. His expression is so sad, and I do the only thing I can think of to soothe him; I hug him tight. He acknowledges it by doing the same and reciprocating, running the tip of his nose across my hairline while inhaling deeply. "Are you sure?"

"Yes. Please find Uncle and take him home."

They're gone right after, and I'm left with a horrified expression. "Uncle Roberto and Silla? You know them?"

"Precious, do you know where my uncle is being kept? Silla?"

Arching my neck back, I meet his questioning gaze. "I don't know where *she* is, but Roberto's here. Hurt, but here."

"Why do you say *she* like that?"

"Because that horrible woman was banned from our lands by my mother more than a century ago for attempting to kill her."

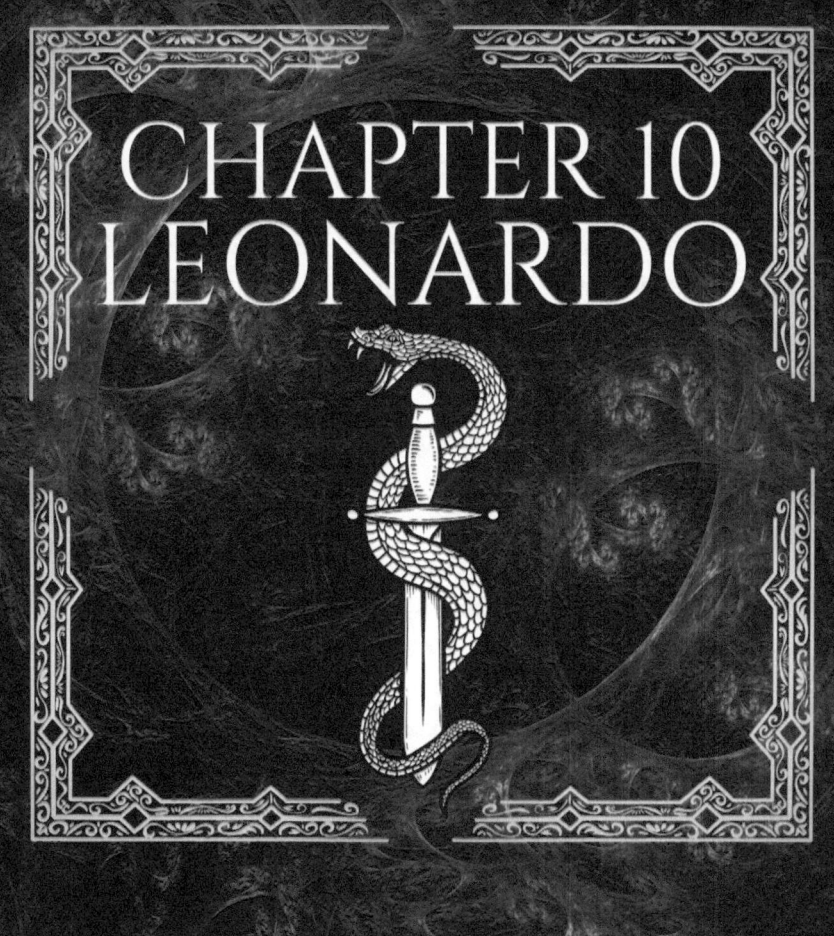

CHAPTER 10
LEONARDO

"Take me to him." The urgency in my tone has her stepping back, but not out of fear. Instead, Anaya holds out her hand for me to take while my prisoners are removed and all but one of my guards head home. He remains close but gives his king and soon-to-be queen enough room to have a semblance of privacy.

That ends, though, when Gabriella and Theodore approach us. Their vampiric speed startles Anaya, our bond signaling the short-lived distress, but it's gone as soon as it arrives.

Anaya gives my sister a small smile while hiding her apprehension, the fear of a reproach she hasn't earned holding her captive. It'll take time and our trust to break that habit; her father's crimes are not hers, and this will be her first lesson.

She doesn't speak, letting the former take the lead, something my sister does in true Gabriella fashion.

When we were children, Gabby was the outspoken one, while Isa held the motherly instincts. She's a little brash and always bold, and this time is no different as she steps up to my mate's other side, taking her other hand in one of hers. That's her acceptance of her.

End of. No questions.

My precious one exhales, the tension draining from her. "I'll show you the way. It's higher up."

"After you, Princess Anaya."

"King Astor." She begins to bow her head, but before I can stop her, Theo shakes his head. He's watching her without malice; I see anger, but it's not directed at her. "I'm confused, Leonardo. Is this not how you greet other royals?"

While I'm happy she's comfortable enough to ask me questions, I hate that she's been subjected to certain things. For one, her father was a misogynistic prick who didn't value his wife, much less his daughter. I'm sure she bowed her head or kneeled—the latter is a humiliating tradition—for the males of her family and men like Brice, who held positions of power.

And while her kingdom found these things acceptable, we don't. We are equals. Respect each other.

"You don't bow to family, sweetheart."

She tilts her head in my direction, still not following me. "My family does...did..." Anaya's genuinely confused and bites her lips, letting out a small sigh "...I don't know what to do."

"They no longer matter," Gabriella answers this time, leaning over a bit so she could look at her husband. "Right, love?"

The vampire nods, smiling at his beloved. "To the family, I'm simply Theo. No title."

"Can I do the same?"

It's an open question I answer by bending my head and pressing a kiss to her temple. "You can do whatever you wish. No need to ask permission."

The responding smile I'm gifted is the most beautiful vision. She's striking, even if still timid. "Then to mine, I want to be simply Aya."

"Aya it is, then."

"Perfect. It's what my mother called me." So much wistfulness. The bond tugs at my chest with her emotions. "Now, let's go see Roberto. I've done what I can, but he needs help."

"What exactly did they do to him?" Theodore asks, his brows furrowed. He caught her apprehension—genuine fear and it's not for herself, but the prisoner.

"They took everything from him."

WE ENTER THE ELEVATOR, and it's bloodied inside—as if someone was shot or lost a limb—but no one mentions it. Instead, we silently watch Anaya press a button on the panel, effectively shutting us inside, and ascend to the floor right beneath the top.

The ride is short, but the walk down these halls is not.

There are dead bodies everywhere, tossed about the deeper we walk as if a beast ran rampant, and the claw marks across their chest and the walls indicate werewolves. If it was Xadiel or another, it makes no difference as we cross over each corpse in silence, and to her credit, my mate doesn't make a sound as the fae body count rises. She swallows hard and shudders, but there are no other outward signs of her true distress.

We sense it, though.

The vampires can scent it, while her emotions are mine, and the saddest part is I'm not sure she understands this. That there's nothing she can hide from me. There will never be any privacy between us.

"It's at the end of this hall. The room on the right." Her voice echoes, a sweet little cadence that causes my cock to throb. My body's reactions to hers are automatic; I feel no guilt over this and let my eyes linger over her lithe frame. She's curvy yet petite, and I find that so tempting—a fantasy turned reality—I love that she's shorter than me.

I can tuck her against my chest for a cuddle or toss her across my bed and fuck her into our mating bed; Anaya is my version of literal perfection with her long, blonde hair and heart-shaped face. Her curves are tucked beneath the mounds of fabric hiding her from the world; I'd felt those child-bearing hips earlier and scented her arousal, two things I could never live without.

Not now. Not ever.

"Do you wish to wait here?" I ask, rubbing my thumb across her knuckles in a gentle sweeping motion. I want her, my cock aching to simply slide across her slit, but her comfort comes before my desires. "We'll grab him and—"

"He trusts me." End of. My mate exhales roughly and straightens her spine, not allowing me to argue those words. There are unshed tears in her violet eyes, though, not that she allows them to fall. Instead, she shifts her attention from me to Gabriella and mouths *I'm sorry* to each of us.

I don't understand it. None of us do, and the confusion is clear as day on our faces, but we're not given the chance to ask. My mate walks ahead of me, having let go of my hand, and straight toward the mentioned room where a guard comes into our line of sight.

He's shaking, ashen while holding a high-caliber rifle at us. It's the same kind the other fae soldiers used downstairs, the translucent bullets inside the magazine visible, and his laser points at Anaya's chest.

"I'll shoot, Princesse. I will not be killed."

"Step out of the way and stand down, Soldier." The authority that pours from my female in those last two words makes him stumble a bit. His brows furrow and his knees shake, but the weapon remains on her. "I'm giving you a chance here, Soldier. Don't add to the body count. Lower your weapon and leave while you can."

"Your father would—"

"He's dead." The news unsettles the man, every bit of blood draining from his face as shock settles in. His lips open and close. Whatever he wants to say is trapped by the news. "And before you ask, Ruben will follow shortly. My father's reign is over."

"No. I do not believe you." Emotional; the fae guard's state of mind is questionable at best. His finger slips and the gun unloads a single bullet that wheezes by an unmoving Anaya, shocking them both. There's a part of him that repents immediately—he's loyal to the fae court—but this mistake cannot be forgiven. "What the fuck!"

My need to protect her overrides everything else, and I'm beside him before anyone realizes I've become invisible and rematerialized. His throat is in my hands and I'm lifting him clear off the ground, feet dangling as he splutters and claws at my hands. The minute damage he's making almost makes me laugh, more so when his face becomes a bit swollen and red from the pressure.

"You dare to shoot at my mate? To almost hurt her?" It leaves me on a hiss, my teeth bared at the man as the tenuous hold I've kept on my anger slips, letting Anaya see all of me unrestrained. For her sake, I've controlled the urges the magic in my veins calls for.

To fuck her. To kill for her.

I've wanted to eradicate her brother and the guard bitch since they first tried to grab for her, but those doe eyes and her scared expression had me reeling the urges back. But not this time. The call for blood burns me, and no cardinal sin could be bigger than trying to harm my mate.

"Please! Princesse, help me!" he gurgled, his spittle flying everywhere. "I'm—"

"Do you wish to spare his life?" My eyes penetrate hers; I await her command. One she gives with a minute shake of her head, and I'm proud of her for understanding that a threat to one is a threat to all. That his attempt on her life, intentional or not, cannot be forgiven. "So be it."

With my unoccupied hand, I pull the opal dagger from my back pocket and flick it open. Its blade glints under the bright lighting seconds before I embed the tip just beneath his chin and up into his skull with one hard shove. At once, blood pools in his mouth and falls, creating another stain on my trousers.

Everything for him slows after...

His breathing. His functions.

Good riddance.

Dropping him to the ground, I pull out my dagger and clean the remnants of his sanguine mess off the sharp blade with two quick swipes across my pants. I watch Anaya for any discomfort at the sight, yet her furrowed brows aren't from disgust or fear, curiosity brims through our bond.

"What is it, precious?"

"Where did you get that? Have you had it this whole time?" I'm nodding as Gabriella and Theo pass us, silently walking into the room, both giving me nods of approval. The guard is kicked out of the way by the vampire king before the door opens and closes and it's just us.

"I have. Xadiel gave it to me."

"How did he come to have this? It's been missing—"

"Do you recognize it?"

"Leonardo, that opal blade has been in my family for genera-tions. It was stolen from my mother's coffers years before I was born. She always lamented losing the gift handed down from her great-grandmother and meant for me later in life." I'm shocked by that, but more so when she takes it from me and swipes her thumb across the hilt. At her touch, a series of curves appear in a cerulean blue shade that matches the aura I met hours earlier. They're slow, as if from disuse, coming together to create a singular word: Anaya. The look on my face, whatever she finds there, causes her to giggle. "Every owner's name appears on the hilt when it's passed down after the previous holder's death. It's a tradition on my maternal side."

"So this is yours?"

"It is." Lovingly, she holds it to her chest. "This carries the essence of every queen before my mother, while hers is the strongest. We feed our blood to the dagger on the day we receive it, binding ourselves to each other."

"I believe you."

That surprises her, the shock clear on her face. "I've felt it for years. This inexplicable connection to it—as if it's a part of me."

"You kept it safe."

"Yes, which makes sense." Bending a bit at the waist, I place a small kiss at the corner of her smiling lips, catching her off guard. Pink blooms across her cheeks at the action, the blush so sweet. So innocent. "Every part of you is mine, precious one. It came to me because it knew someday we'd meet and I'd be able to see this gorgeous smile sweep over your face."

Her grin only widens, a tiny hint of fang peeking through. "You're a smooth talker, aren't you?"

"Only with you."

"Yeah, you're going to be trouble all right." There's mischief in her eyes, a lightness that wasn't there earlier before she places the knife back in my hand. "Hold it for me. I know it's secure with you."

"Always. It'd be my honor." That trust makes me feel a hundred feet tall.

"Thank you." Her head tilts then, and Anaya's about to say something else, hopefully a little sassy as I enjoy this side of her, but then a scream rends the air. Our heads whip in the direction of the door, the high shrieks of fear turning into muffled sobs, and she takes off before I have a chance to stop her.

The door bangs open from the force and I'm right on her heels, but stop in my tracks at the sight that greets me. If a moment ago I felt pride, right now, I'm an asshole.

So ashamed of myself.

The man I thought to be a disgrace—a traitor to his kind—is emaciated and shackled by the ankle. Infection is contained to that area, but you can see the toll it's had on his body. *How long has it been like this?* No man, mortal or other can survive a hundred years like this.

His body is bruised and broken from years of abuse. Then, there's the vacancy in his eyes, as if he doesn't understand reality and is lost within the stronghold of his fear. Uncle Roberto's attention doesn't waver from the wall opposite of him, the same place that Gabriella and Theodore are plastered against while she holds a hand to her mouth.

This is my father's brother.

This is what we allowed.

Uncle Roberto is dirty, yet his scent lingers. So much like our father's but with notes of sweet citrus that weren't there the last time I saw him. It's a bit cloying. Causes my nose to twitch, but I don't dare move and further unsettle him.

"Anaya, maybe you should—" All noises coming from him cease at the mention of her name. As if a veil of calm overtakes him, Roberto lays back and mouths her name.

Over and over.

In a plea. As a form of comfort.

"I'm here, Berto. Please calm down." She kneels beside his cot, not caring in the least about the dirty mess all around him. There's old, moldy food and what seems like piss in a bucket and Gods know what else...she doesn't hesitate to aid him. "I'm here. Just breathe with me."

Anaya places her hands on either side of his temples and starts a slow rhythmic sequence he's slow to follow. There are four seconds between each breath, a continuous loop our uncle succumbs to and then falls asleep on the tenth cycle.

My mate doesn't pull away yet, though. Her powers come alive as he rests, the soft glow of her hands against his skin bringing a bit of life to his body.

Roberto's cheeks become less gaunt, his ribs less noticeable, and a light sheen of pink touches his cheek. She's doing this, reminding me of what I'd paid little attention to but Brice made sure to point out.

You've been holding out on us, ma princesse. That's going to cost you.

"You're a healer."

Anaya doesn't pull her attention from my uncle; she concentrates and gives until she teeters atop him. It's then I step in. I'm just close enough to catch her as she passes out, but I still manage to hear her.

Faint. Shaky.

"I am."

CHAPTER 11
Anaya

I come awake again, sitting astride Leonardo's lap with my head tucked against his chest. He's talking to someone, the deep baritone of his voice almost lulling me back to sleep, but then I realize we're moving.

Much the way fae do when flying, there's this feeling of exhilaration that crawls up my skin, and I can't help the giddy smile that stretches across my lips from the sensation. It's not strong, but there and welcomed and I'm ready to pop off his lap and investigate when whatever we're on gives a little dip.

My eyes snap open with urgency, the jolt sending a shock

through my system, and I'm reminded of my weakened state when the world spins around me. I can't make out faces or what we're in, but I feel like we're high up in the sky. Can't shake the sensation. It's been so long for me.

We can soar with the beasts that roam the sky—it's in our nature to want to frolic and feel the air caress our wings—but my father outlawed any form of flying unless you were part of his aerial military unit. And even then, it's limited to what he deems—deemed —necessary.

"I'm going to need to get used to that," I mutter low, rubbing my closed fist over my left eye and then my right, my vision still a bit blurry. In the last few weeks, I've healed myself, Isabella, and now Roberto.

The latter did me in.

I've been taking care of him for years, slowly nurturing him back into a somewhat healed state when I can, but never to this degree. I felt it the moment we touched; death was knocking at his door, but it wasn't his time. I'd never be able to help him otherwise.

Fate cannot be challenged. The date of your death is preordained, and no amount of magic or luck will change it.

"Get used to what, precious?"

"You calling me that, for starters." I blink again, and his eyes are the only thing I can make out. They're striking, such a beautiful shade of blue—nearly identical to my aura—and a replica of the shadowed figure from my dream. "I've dreamed of these before."

"Of what?" he says, and for a second we shift, my weight being lifted as he moves us somewhere else. Those he'd been talking to carry on. I can faintly make out the voice of his other sister asking a question about a large tree. "Explain."

"Where are we?" I ask instead as we seem to step into another room, and when the door closes, all noises cease. It's just the two of us. "This feels different."

"We're heading home, little mate." His lips brush my hairline a second before we dip, the surface we're on contorting to our combined weight, and then I'm settled over his chest. Heat rises from my head to my toes and I feel my face blush, but this only pulls a chuckle from him. "Comfortable?"

"Yes."

"Good." His large hand comes up to cradle the back of my head and he pushes it toward his chest, softly scratching the back of my head. It feels so good, but at the same time, I don't want to stop seeing his eyes. I need to have them on mine, so I shift just enough to the side that I'm able to enjoy him and lay half on him and half on the bed.

"I don't want to miss anything," I say in way of explanation, which he replies to with a raised brow. "My eyesight isn't working well at the moment. I depleted myself." Which reminds me. I sit up and twitch my nose, ignoring the sudden wave of dizziness that rolls through me from the quick movement. I can't scent anyone but him at the moment, and I know I heard his sister's voice. *How much damage did I cause myself?* "Where's Berto? You didn't leave—"

"Relax, sweetheart."

"But—"

"Come here." Leonardo uses my...*shirt*? At the perplexed expression on my face, the warlock king pulls me onto my side and lies in front of me, face to face with our legs intertwined so I have a better view of his eyes. His hands caress me, slow rhythmic strokes that calm my bout of panic, and I'm brought down after a few minutes. I'm pliant and a bit lulled when he begins to speak. "I'm going to begin explaining a few things first, and then I expect the same from you. Always honest, remember?"

"Please."

"First, Gabriella changed you out of your dress as it was filthy and torn in a few places." Before I can ask where it is, I feel him place a finger over my lips. He's still blurry, but I can make out the top of his cheeks now. "We didn't throw it away; it's in a bag for you to do as you please with when we arrive, but we thought you'd be more comfortable in something of mine. My shirt and sweatpants are adorable on you. Big and swallow you up, but I think you look beautiful in them."

"I've never worn anything other than dresses before." This causes me to blush again. It's his clothing I'm wearing, something I find myself excited about, but in the same breath, I'm admitting my lack of self-autonomy. That I've grown up not having choices. "It feels different."

"Good or bad?" No judgment in his tone. So much understanding. "And I apologize if you feel we took—"

"It's good, Leonardo. Very good."

"To my loved ones, I'm just Leo. No need for formalities, Anaya." He snuggles in a little closer, his breath skimming my lips. "Please relax around us. We're not going to hurt you."

"I'm not afraid of you or your family."

"Then say, *Leo*. You're the only person alive with the right to call me anything you want."

"What if I like saying your name? What if it gives me butterflies?" It's easier to admit this since my vision hasn't fully come back yet. Yes, I get to enjoy the warmth of his eyes—how I saw them before we met is still a mystery to me—but this is intimate. Our cozy bubble makes me happy. "Would you still prefer otherwise?"

"No."

"Why?"

"Because what makes you happy fills that space inside my chest that's been empty for so long." Again, he begins combing his hand through my hair. He brings one of his large hands to my hairline and pushes flyaways back, then tucks other strands behind my ear. This goes on for a while. It feels so good, and every so often it's accompanied by the stroke of two fingers across my cheek. "And to answer your earlier question, Roberto's resting and looks so much better thanks to you. He woke up once, but this time he recognized me, and after getting him to drink some water, he went back to sleep. Gabriella is watching him now."

A bit of the stress I'd been carrying for Berto melts away. "I was happy to help."

"But you overdid it, Anaya." Leonardo's tone gets a bit rough, a tinge of anger to it, and I don't like it. Everything in me demands I fix it. Make him smile again. *The mate bond between us is so strong already; I feel his concern. His true wish is to keep me close.* "Never put yourself in danger like that."

"I don't like you being upset with me."

It's a bit confusing. Being told about a bond and experiencing it are two very different things.

Maybe it's the fact I lived so long with the emptiness of thinking my mate was dead that broke something in me. Maybe it's watching my father treat my mother like dirt under his shoe that makes Leonardo's care and open emotions an enigma.

Yet I wouldn't change him.

I feel the ties between us now fully, and the longer we're in each other's presence, the stronger they become. Like a threadbare string that wrapped itself around my heart, but the more the organ pumps— it sings for him—the more solid the binding. We've gone from a feeling, this shock where we touch, to being irrevocably bound.

"I'm not mad at you, Anaya. Just the situation." He exhales roughly, his sweet breath tickling my nose and I twitch, causing him to chuckle. "Are you complaining?"

"That's better. Smile more."

"You're going to be trouble." At that, my eyes mock glare while he moves his head back just a bit and copies my action. "What did you say about my eyes earlier?"

"It will probably make me sound insane." I'm starting to feel lethargic and I yawn, keeping my small fangs behind my lips. He hasn't noticed yet, and I'm shy about them. Being a royal, mine are slightly more pointed than other fae females. "But I've dreamed of them once. I was alone in my mother's garden at home, and a shadow watched over me; its eyes were just like yours. Same beautiful blue."

"Interesting."

"How so?" Another yawn, but I still manage to bring a hand up to his face and press my open palm against his cheek. My vision is still hazy, but I can make out his nose with a slight bump over the bridge now and those perfect lips that stretch into a dazzling smile. "Did you dream of me?"

"I'm starting to think the dagger gave me a part of you years ago. Before your birth even."

"Maybe the gods were paving the way for us, Leonardo." More yawning. I'm burrowing deeper into the pillow under my head, watching him through a now loopy gaze. "Giving us hope."

"You truly like using my birth name, don't you?"

"Yes."

"Then never stop." Wrapping an arm around my waist, he tugs me closer and intertwines our legs together. My head is against his chest, his decadent scent with a tone of spice relaxing me. "Now sleep, my precious one. We'll be home soon."

THERE'S nothing in particular that wakes me this time, but when I do open my eyes everything comes into focus. I'm in a room with large, arched windows that nearly reach the ceiling, the stained-glass paneling at the top blocking out a bit of the evening light peeking through the trees. Because I'm surrounded; nature vibrates and thrives on these lands and within these walls.

I find potted greenery throughout, no matter which way I look, without being overwhelming. It's an aesthetic without trying, but the scent of chocolate is still the predominant note within these walls.

On the sheets covering me.

In the air I breathe.

I can feel it. Sense him in every single part of this bedroom.

It's an open space with a king-size bed and a tufted headboard in the same tone of dark teal as the walls. There's a harmony in it, not pretentious nor boring, but more of a lived-in luxury that pulls a happy sigh from me.

There are gold accents throughout to break up the singular note: in a large, ornate golden-framed mirror, the sconces on the wall, and the one piece of artwork with a frame that seems older than I've been alive, delicate and with detailed filigree.

It's gothic beauty, but where is the owner?

That's who I want to see and without a second thought, I throw the covers off and slip over the edge of the tall bed. A tiny jump and I'm on the ground, finding a pair of warm slippers just steps from me. They're big, but they work, and I head out the door a minute later after fixing my hair into a low bun at the base of my neck.

Without the use of modern technology in my realm, women used old techniques to style and curl their hair, while my mother taught me the advantages of wrapping your hair a certain way to create loose waves every time. I never used heat, but humid locks and a few bobby pins held it all together for me.

It's what I do now but with the use of a rubber band this time. Leonardo had one on the left side of his bedside table near a well-read book on alchemy. The pages were a little bent, the cover faded but well-kept and used.

Once I step outside the room, I notice I'm on the second floor with a grand staircase a few feet from me. There's a bustle below, the shuffling of feet and the drum of conversations in passing, and I wonder how many people live here with him.

On his territory. Part of the royal coven.

Unlike the fae who mostly live in or close to our court, Wiccans choose to migrate and form small communities with others of their kind. Yet this is home, as much as the royal court will always call to me.

Peering over the banister, I descend a few steps in hopes of catching a glimpse of anyone I know. Unfortunately, what I find are women and men whom I've never seen and who turn their heads in my direction as I continue down. They don't speak to me, expressions neutral where they stand, and I can't help but want to run and hide.

"Quit staring," a voice calls out, and an older woman steps through the growing crowd. They seem to be multiplying as I reach the final step, varying in ages and dressed in different uniforms. From men dressed like the guards who helped us back in Canada, to maids, and some who look like they're simply visiting or passing through. "His Highness will not be happy to find everyone in here acting this way. Back to whatever you were doing."

"But she's a *fae*, Mrs. Isotta." This comes from a young witch dressed in a figure-hugging black dress that ended mid-thigh, the bell sleeves long and flowy. She's beautiful on the outside with dark hair and ample curves, but something about her gives off an off-putting feel. Her vibrations are dark. "What is a traitor to the crown doing in our king's home? In his clothes?"

There's a possessive look on her face. The jealousy in her whiny voice makes me believe she's someone to the warlock king, and I don't like it.

"I'm Leonardo's guest." Gasps come from those around me at the blatant use of his name; I will not back down either. I've spent all my life hiding and looking down and afraid of my own shadow—no more. He claimed me as his, and I feel the bond tug at me now as I stand here, my distress turning into annoyance at this witch's attempt to rile up the crowd here against me.

I know who I am. Who my father was.

But that doesn't mean I will live my life paying for every broken plate the man has stacked against him.

"How dare you! Show some respect and address him by his title."

"Miss Chiara, that's enough. You are no one here to question our king or his guest."

"Her kind cannot be trusted." At her words, murmurs grow. Stares become more penetrating, but I find relief in the lack of hostility. Curious? Yes. Hold trepidation? Also yes, but no hate outside of this Chiara woman who likes to hear herself speak. "Or do we not remember what happened to our prior—"

"King Larue's daughter owes no one a damn thing. Not me. Not any of you." Leonardo stalks toward me, eyes smoldering as he gives my short frame a heated roam from head to toe. He's sweating and the black cotton shirt clings to his muscles, a few specks of blood coating his cheek and I know they're not his. The blood has a tinge of dark blue to it. *Fae.* Behind him, Gabriella and Theodore follow and they're both glaring at the witch. "She is my mate. My queen."

Gasps erupt from the crowd, but they don't argue. If anything, I'm examined more closely—I should feel shy under the scrutiny—but my attention is on the blood I smell on him. My nose and ears twitch the closer he gets, and I can now make out the owners of the sanguine drops marking his clothes and cheek. There's also no mistaking Brice or Ruben's stench.

Am I a horrible person for not caring about them? If they live or die?

"How can you accept her? Her father killed—"

"This coming from the offspring of a traitorous warlock?" Gabriella comes and stands to the other side of me, her support clear. "Or did you forget that I was best friends with Lilibeth? That I was her confidant before she betrayed our people—my family—for a few gold coins?"

"I-I don't know what you're talking about. My sister didn't do anything." Chiara looks around for support, and only one woman steps up beside her. They're family; it's clear as day in the facial similarities. "We were framed and hunted by vampires. It's all lies."

"So you're calling *me* a liar now," Theodore's voice thunders as he stares her down, his eyes burning bright red. "That I killed every one of those bastards because I needed to find amusement?"

She doesn't answer the vampire king, even as her legs shake under his wrathful stare. She's afraid. Reeks of it, but Chiara changes her expression from viper to demure in the blink of an eye. Tries to sway my mate with a small smile. "My king, I did not come here to fight. Please, let's all calm down and discuss our union—"

"Enough of your bullshit, Chiara. Leave." If Theodore's voice scared a few of the witches here, Leonardo's command has them bowing their necks. Those two words hold the command of their king to the fullest extent, and she buckles under the pressure. "You are no longer welcome at my home. On my lands."

With a whimper caught in her throat, Chiara looks down and then turns away from us, but not before glaring at me. The ill intent is there. Her dislike of me is blatant, but beneath it, there's a woman who feels wronged somehow.

As if I stole from her.

"Who is she to you, Leonardo?"

CHAPTER 12
LEONARDO

A naya has been asleep for the last two days now, her body finally succumbing to the exhaustion she's been cat-napping through for goddess knows how long. She needs it, though.

Between healing my uncle, something she's done often if the conditions we found him in are anything to go by—and what happened in Canada—my mate's been running on empty. We watched her gift a part of her aura to save his life, something that left her unable to care for herself as she passed out in my arms. Gabriella changed her and washed her face, making me aware of bruising in a few areas of her body.

They've abused her. Hit her.

And yet, she's proven twice that she'd jump into the fire to save someone else instead of protecting herself. Anaya didn't have to expose her gift because of a few split knuckles on my hand, but she did. It wasn't necessary, and I wanted to be angry at her, but it's nearly impossible to do so when she looks at me with those warm, violet doe eyes of hers.

When she says my name in that sweet, breathy tone.

Not Leo. Not some nickname or "Your Highness," nothing but my goddess-given name.

Moreover, the irony lies in the fact I've never been a fan of it, the formality in which people say it, but on her lips, it sounds sexy. Sinful. More so after she admits it gives her butterflies each time.

"I'm in trouble with this one."

"Did you say something, Your Highness?" Augusto asks from beside me, his mustache twitching. "Who's in trouble?"

"Mind your business, old man."

"I'm not old. The missus says I'm distinguished; there's a difference."

"She lied to you." We're a few feet from the jail and the two guards standing at the post bow their heads in greeting. They don't move or blink, watching the perimeter for anyone—trespassers— more so since our newest addition entered the building.

There's been no word on the fallout from the fae realm or the actions the court will take, something I know Anaya worries about. She mumbled about it last night during a fitful sleep, tossing and turning a few times while the words *heir* and *war* were on repeat.

I calmed her down as best I could, but the root of the issue would not go away that easily. Nor will I release their new king to wreak havoc on my people or that of my sister's.

The well-lit floor opens to a desk where a woman mans the

station today. Her demeanor is serious as we walk closer until a large smile breaks out across her face.

"Your Highness."

"Mrs. Augusto." My greeting earns me a snort from her mate and an eye roll from her. It's been the same since I was a kid, choosing to mess with his mate and her getting me back by withholding my favorite pastries as retaliation. "Anything new to report?"

Her mate walks past me and around the desk she mans, giving her a quick kiss on the cheek. She smiles at him before dropping the amusement and typing a few things into her computer.

Over the years, I've updated our systems, from adding solar to aid our power grid, to installing internet access for everyone who lives here. We've adapted, as have all other beings, learning to navigate this new world that humans have created.

For money, I've invested over the years in hotels and large resorts along the Italian coast. That, and a few Michelin-starred restaurants located at the epicenter of our major tourist destinations.

I've also partnered with Xadiel in a few infrastructure projects the government has ordained. Years of success have brought in more than enough money to take care of those who call our royal lands home.

To pay them well for the jobs they hold, which are invaluable to keep this place running. From this jail to the on-site hospital and a school, my people have everything they could need within reach.

It's something I watched my father do, but Xadiel perfected it. You encourage those under your aegis to grow and open stores—to become self-reliant business owners while catering to the growing needs of newer generations.

I've expanded our territory.

A full city is hidden within the depths of a charmed forest with protection spells against outside visitors. Unless you are welcomed onto our lands, you'll never find our home.

Annett and Augusto are two of those people. She's incredibly smart, a quick-witted and skilled fighter. He's my right hand, someone I trust completely.

Annett turns her monitor around so I can see the video coming from Ruben's cell. He's yelling and trying to use his magic, the initial attempts of conjuring a portal are there but to his failure, and he begins to destroy the little we allowed to be kept in the room.

The toilet attached to the wall has been kicked until it broke, creating a water problem for the floor. The small water fountains for each room have been turned off and so has the septic system. Maintenance was called in to fix the issue, and he tried to fight my employee and escape but was tasered and subdued instead.

"He was transferred to the lower levels?"

"Yes, my king."

"And the other one?" I'd spent time with him yesterday, taking out my aggression on the man who thought it right to try to force my mate into a bond she didn't want. "Is he awake?"

"He is." Annett smirks. "He's angry at being moved from his cell and into the same one as Prince Ruben."

"Thank you, Annett. I'll be heading down now."

"Happy interrogation, Your Highness."

Tapping my knuckles on her desk, I turn and head for the stairwell leading into the lower levels. While the top floors are sophisticated and run with modern touches to give dignity to those serving a sentence, the underground dungeon is primitive by comparison. These floors are lit by torches and magic, the rooms are held by barriers that stop prisoners from escaping in painful ways, and for these two, we've treated them to a healthy dose of iron.

The bars. The bed frame. The bowls in which water is provided all have just enough to hurt, but not kill. This specific metal is harmful to their kind, and the bloodshot eyes that greet me say they're feeling the full extent.

"Good after, gentlemen," I greet, and Brice rushes toward us, only to be thrown back by the door's ward. His body slams into the rock wall, and he grunts in pain as he lands on his side. He's slow to get up, too, limping a bit from his left leg. "That looked painful. I don't suggest you do that again."

"Fuck you." His hiss is followed by a scream; he touches a solid iron pipe on the floor. Almost tripped again from the sharp jolt of pain. Like silver hurts werewolves, this metal kills the fae in a very painful way. "Let me out and fight me like a man."

"Or I can always come to you." Stepping through, I crane my head from side to side while motioning with my hand for him to attack. "Let's continue where we left off."

The last word hasn't left my lips when the brute rushes me with everything he has left in him. I won't deny he's a skilled fighter, but it's all brawn and very little brains. There's not much strategy in use, throwing his body weight against me, and I use the momentum to flip our positions and land on top of him. He bucks beneath me and tries hard to throw me off, but the elbow to his neck causes him to choke.

I add pressure to his windpipe, nearly crushing it, but then pull back and stand. I'm looking down at him as he tries to desperately get air in, rubbing the area with a large and nearly all-black bruised hand.

Yesterday, I'd beaten both with a hammer after Gabriella described the splotches of purples and green on Anaya's hips; she saw them when she'd changed her. I didn't ask questions or interrogate or even explain how things work. I swung until satisfied and then walked out.

It looks like someone purposely dug their fingers in and burned her.

And I'd bet my crown he did that. Hurt an innocent woman for his sick perversion.

"Get up." A solid kick to the midsection has him choking again, a coughing/hacking fit following. My head turned toward his prince. "Is this who leads your military?"

"You cannot continue to hold us prisoner, witch. This is an act of war."

I'm in front of him in an instant, face to face with no space between us. He's shackled to the ceiling after his earlier display, stripped of his dignity, too, since he soiled his clothes by breaking that toilet and causing flooding issues.

The grip I have on his face is tight and he grunts in pain when my blunt fingernails break skin on his chin. "So was killing my father and mother...innocent people. Or did you conveniently forget about that?"

"He suffers from selective memory, my king. Most pieces of shit do."

"Such stupidity." Releasing him, I pivot and his general slams right into Ruben's ribs, the force dislocating his shoulder. It snapped back hard, but with no give in his shackles, the bone became misaligned.

"Merde!" His scream pierces, very high in pitch. "You idiot! Fucking shit, that hurts."

"Quit crying," Brice seethes, wiping blood off his lip but more falls. It's split at the center, and only a healer with a steady hand will fix it. I'm not providing that. Don't believe in wasting money or resources. "I've taken the worst of it."

"No. You haven't." Holding a hand out, I wait for Augusto to place a leather whip in my open palm. The robust material grips well. I've had this one made for punishment with a pattern on the hilt for non-slippage.

I give a test snap of my hand and it lands on the general's hand, splitting the skin open at the center. This time his screams fill the room, quickly followed by the prince's.

For each strike I unleash, the other gets an equal lash.

"Where is Silla?" I ask from between clenching teeth, brandishing another direct hit over Brice's right flank this time. I'm spreading each one out, leaving a trail of welts beneath the torn shirts each man is wearing. "Who helped her?"

The woman Angelo named Lilou, who paid them to infiltrate my kingdom, is dead. I saw Isabella end her, but I'm sure Lilou didn't act alone, that one of these two helped.

"Don't. Know." Brice breathes through the pain a little better than Ruben. He's more alert, too. "I have no idea who that is."

"And Lilou?" That gets me a reaction. A bit of pain, but mostly anger. "What is she to you?"

"Dead." It's hissed out, the spittle staining my black shirt. There's a tinge of blue to it, the dual tone almost making it appear violet. "My sister is dead because of your whore—" The insult is cut off by a single slice across the face with the tip of my whip. Pain explodes behind his processors; it's etched on his face, and the eyelid I'd managed to nick swells immediately.

He doesn't speak. Doesn't move.

Yet his dark brown wings unfurl and wrap around him for protection—the sight of a broken pride. And while I'm not a cruel man, no part of me holds remorse for him.

Not for the death of his sister or his future, when he was a willing participant in Anaya's cruel surroundings.

"You have enemies far more dangerous than us, King Leonardo." Ruben's head hangs from between his shoulders, his blood dripping from open wounds staining my floor. "From within."

"All rulers do, Ruben. I'm not afraid."

"For her, you should be." The *her* is Anaya, and the blood in my veins heats at the threat. I've been dangling from a precipice for so long, wanting my revenge, but everything takes a back seat when it comes to her. My mate. "Silla's formidable. Cunning." His chuckle turns into a cough mid-laugh, his body shaking from the pain. It takes a minute, but he manages to gather himself and look up. His eyes are haunted, yet I find no remorse. "You know she is. She fooled you all once, and a snake in the grass always has friends. Mow your lawn, Wiccan king, and watch your steps."

That's all I get from him, the questions on the tip of my tongue going unanswered as a second later, Prince Ruben passes out.

PRESENT...

"WHO IS SHE TO YOU, LEONARDO?" There's a bit of an accusation in her tone, but Anaya keeps her expression neutral. She also waits until everyone has left, including our family, before asking, "Why did she seem so possessive over a man who has a mate?"

"It's not what you're thinking, my mate." I'm holding two hands up as I turn to face her, my smirk turning into a full-blown grin. How can I not when I feel her jealousy through our bond? When the physical proof is staring me down with annoyance. *She's too adorable.* "That witch is someone I want nothing to do with. Have never given her the time of day, no matter how much she's wanted differently."

"She's possessive of you, and I don't like it."

"I belong to you, Aya. You, my precious mate."

"You better." With a huff, she turns and heads back up the stairs while clutching my shorts at the waist. My female is practically swimming in my clothes. "I'm going to shower, then figure out my life choices."

"As you wish," I call out, but get no response. And a second later, it's the softest slam of a door that follows.

Even while being bothered, she holds back.

As her mate, it's my job to break every single bind that holds her back. I'll unleash my precious one while giving her the reassurance she needs.

CHAPTER 13
Anaya

I don't know why it's bothering me so much, but the more time passes, the more irritated I become. We just met, and yet I claim his as mine. I've accepted his claim on me and validated our reactions to one another—the signs of a fated mate have been there since the moment he said *hello*.

But this female witch bothers me.

The look of contempt she gave me before walking out of his home reminds me of the hate I saw in Lilou's eyes, how my mere existence ruined her plans for the future. Brice's sister had plans of grandeur on a reality budget of a mistress, much to her brother's embarrassment.

I heard him chastise her once. Called her a pathetic whore who should aspire to be more like me and less like their mother.

That cut her deep, the hurt plain on her face from my hiding spot behind a pillar. Tears spilled down her cheeks, but Lilou didn't wipe them away as he continued to berate her, and at that moment, her real dislike for me bloomed.

Just like this Chiara woman. Same contempt and ire.

"Was he going to tie himself to her?" My words are lost beneath the overhead waterfall feature in Leonardo's walk-in shower. The almost too-hot water and the pressure feel amazing on my back, as does the perfume of his shower gel. It's bergamot and cinnamon, which only enhances his already delicious scent.

Right now, I feel as though I'm surrounded by him.

"Maybe they knew each other, but she had a crush..." I trail off, rubbing the lather across my chest and lower—from nipples to my swollen clit—and each pass elicits a shiver from me. Every inch of me is sensitive, and I'm curious to explore as the opportunity has never been this safe.

There's no one wanting to take from me. To punish me for their mere enjoyment.

Because I'd be called so much worse than a whore if I'd been caught touching myself back in the fae's realm; my father would've had me publicly flogged to cleanse me of sin. Not because we're a prudish people. It's quite the opposite. Faes are known to be insatiable lovers who welcome both female and male partners, multiples at that, without there ever being any prejudice from our society.

We accept and are open when it comes to sex—well, everyone but me was allowed to be.

In the eyes of the high court, I'm a doll never to be soiled.

It's why I continue a little lower in this empty shower and stroke across my entrance, almost shocked by the way it clenches on nothing and the feelings it evokes. I feel empty. Needy.

A little more pressure and I slip inside to the first knuckle, closing my eyes as a rush of heat envelops me. Wetness slips from me, and I'm so slick that on the next pump of my finger, I take it fully and moan.

"Sweetest fucking sound in the world." I'm startled by his rough voice, the hunger in it, and let out a small shriek-turned-whimper when I turn around to face him. My male is standing mere inches from me and wearing only a pair of boxer briefs that do little to hide the hard appendage straining against the fabric. He's thick and long, the shape clearly outlined, and the water falling over us only serves to highlight his perfection.

A hard clench has me biting my lip to catch a moan.

It takes a moment for me to speak, but when I do, I'm breathy. My need is clear. "What are you doing in here?"

"I'm exactly where I belong." He steps closer, closing the gap between his body and mine, and when we touch, I feel as though I'm taking my very first breath. It's impossible to put into words what I'm experiencing—how he affects me—yet there's no denying how right this is.

Having him this close.

His skin against mine.

I feel as though I've gone through life without sight or smell until *him*.

"Do you feel it, too?"

"Since the moment your scent slammed into me, I've been yours." Bringing a hand to the back of my neck, Leonardo tilts my head back while he lowers his to meet my lips. Just skims his lips across mine a few times in a feather-light touch that elicits a low, keening sound from me. And he likes it; the heated pools of blue darken and his grip on me tightens while the hardness barely contained by his underwear brushes across my abdomen. "No other woman before you, and there will be no other after, Anaya. My mate has always and will always be my one and only."

"But Chiara...oh *fuck*," I hiss when he wraps his other hand behind my back and lifts me just enough to slip between my thighs, my back against his shower wall. When he lowered his boxer briefs? I do not know or care. Instead, I'm enthralled by the way he's not trying to take me, but rather pressing against my core and flexing, each throb forcing a deep and wanting clench from me. "She said…I watched…oh *Gods* that feels good."

I'm squirming, trying to shift and find the friction from a minute ago. My body is begging for more. For things I've never needed before but right now feel as though I can't live without.

I want this male and understand we're a soul divided that's been reunited. Hunger for him on a carnal level, but what if—

"Listen to me, and listen well, my mate." His words are punctuated by the thrust of his hips against me, the blunt head of his cock separating my labia. They part for him. I'm so wet and swollen, and the only thing I can do is close my eyes and feel. "Open them. I want those violet eyes on me." They do as if his word is law, and I'm rewarded by a quick nip to my bottom lip. "Good girl. Focus on me."

I swallow hard at the praise, liking it. Almost preen. "I'm—"

"I only want you." This time he swipes his tongue over the abused area, and my nipples harden further. The stiff peaks rub against his chest, sending pleasurable shockwaves to my pussy. It's like he has the map and key to my every erogenous zone, unlocking one at a time and I let him, moving my hips over his length without pause or doubt. My body just knows and I follow its lead, discovering with every gyration or touch what I like. "You, Anaya. I've lived over a hundred years knowing that someday my mate would come, and I'd never disrespect or hurt her by desiring another. You will be my first and last. My only."

"Swear it, Leonardo."

"With my life. You're all I'll ever want."

"I accept you." No sooner have the words left me than he turns, ravenous. His gratitude is in the tight way he holds me and the near-desperate slide of his cock through my folds. In the way he slants his mouth over mine, stealing the very breath from my lungs while simultaneously giving me life.

This is my first kiss, and while a part of me is nervous, I can't deny the way it settles my soul. They're contradicting emotions, from one extreme to the other, but the truth:

The way his mouth presses against mine, the soft swipe of his tongue fights for dominance with the hard thrust, and the sinful way the swollen head of his cock kisses my clit with every stroke. Each pass fills me with wonder, and this near-painful teasing leaves me breathless.

A breathlessness I try to bite back, but he doesn't accept that. His tongue slips inside my mouth and caresses mine, twining and stroking at the same pace his girth brings me closer to an edge with a freefall that both excites and scares me.

But then he stops. All of it.

Leonardo pulls back just far enough to look down the front of my body, pausing where he's hard and throbbing. "Fuck, you're beautiful."

"Please." I need him to keep going. I'd never ask him to stop. "More."

"Do you believe me? Understand that I'll never want another?"

"Yes." Almost a sob, that delicious friction that's been building is starting to wane, and that is unacceptable. Hate it. "I believe."

"Then don't you dare hold back again, precious. Let me hear you, Aya." It's a growl against my mouth as he presses our lips together once more as his chest and mine touch. The vibrations cause a shiver to run through me, for my hips to buck, and his head to notch at my entrance. Just sitting there, and the implication and desires—our longing—are the same, and he pushes forward an inch. Just enough that the stretch begins to burn.

Two short strokes, no deeper than just below the bulbous head, and my body clamps down so hard on the tip it's nearly painful. "Take me."

"Not yet, Princess, but soon." From the back of my neck, he moves his hand to the front and gives a light squeeze. "This was not about me today, Anaya. Right now all that matters is you…for you to realize that I'll always take care of you."

"Oh, Gods." There's a lick of heat building from the bottom of my feet and quickly moving up my body. I want to chase it. Own it. "What is this?"

"Us. Simply us."

"Us?" I ask on a whine, trying to shift and take him a little deeper. It works, and I'm gifted another small pump of his hips. I'm thrumming in his hold, whatever is building is close to bursting, and I'm knocked breathless when he brings the hand around my back between us. "Only us."

A press of his thumb against my clit has me losing track of reality as pleasure, unlike anything I could've imagined, slams into me. My eyes close and my body thrashes, and the place between my thighs pulses in time with my rapid heartbeat. Time and reason cease to exist outside of this moment and I'm left a breathless, boneless fae a few minutes later when I stop shaking.

Wetness drips from me and onto him. I feel like I'm marking this male, and my inner fae loves it. *I want to do it again. Bite him where my wetness drips.*

"You can mark me as many times as you want, my queen." There's a hint of amusement in his tone as he answers my unspoken question. It's also then that I notice he's still hard and throbbing. My hand leaves his shoulder and tries to reach down, but he stops me with a peck to the lips and a shake of the head. "Rest, Anaya. We have the rest of our lives to play."

CHAPTER 14
Anaya

"I see the fae bitch is still here, Aunt Lena," a female voice says as her high-heeled shoes enter the kitchen. Everyone in the room looks up, but much to the owner's annoyance, they send a hostile glare her way. In the last week, I've learned that this witch isn't liked among this peaceful coven.

She's too hostile. Too childish.

It rubs the other females wrong, and they've made their complaints known to whom they treat as their queen. Something I've yet to come to grips with. In seven days, my life has changed dramatically—I no longer look over my shoulder or cry myself to sleep.

Instead, I spend my days getting to know the man who saved me. He's sweet. Talkative when it comes to me and a no-nonsense leader for his people. Not cruel or mean—he's giving while also keeping those who live here protected.

He helps those outside of this coven, too. Talking and messaging through his computer, always available to be an ear or settle disputes —walk through a portal and bless those new additions to his kingdom.

Then, there are those who choose to live on these lands. From the old to the young, and my favorites, the kitchen staff—they've made me feel more than at home.

I've never been allowed to cook before, but they indulge my questions and desire to learn. They don't restrict my diet, either.

My meals are just like everyone else's, and the changes in my body have been positive. I'm glowing and smiling; my ribs are padded with enough flesh that they no longer poke out the sides and give me a gaunt appearance.

I'm happier than ever, but this woman has the ability to cause my beautiful bubble to pop.

"That she is, my child." The older of the two, the same woman who stood by Chiara's side as Leonardo banished her last week, looks down her nose at me. She has the same sour look on her face, too. Yet if they only knew that to me *they* reek, a little like garbage, and a lot like a cloying vanilla perfume. "Some women just have no self-respect."

"Didn't my mate kick you out of his lands? Why are you here?" I ask, causing a few of the women in the kitchen to chuckle. I've gotten to know them. Spent some time helping around the house— even when they kicked me out or asked me to sit down because I was a special guest—I enjoyed our every interaction. "Should I call him?"

"Go ahead, Miss Larue. Please do so, and tell him the Rossi coven is here." Chiara's too cocky, but I find it peculiar that she doesn't say *she's* here but uses the name of her coven. "Or do you need me to do it for you?"

"Please seat yourselves in the living room. Someone will bring you refreshments." It's easy, but I fall right back into the role my father drilled into me. Pleasant. Fake smile. "Anything in particular you'd like to drink?"

"Water or a Coke is fine."

I can feel the questioning gaze of those around me, the ones who matter, but I ignore them and wave the guests out of the kitchen. And while they walk, their heels clacking against the flooring, I pull out the cell phone Leonardo bought me a few days after we arrived.

"Anaya, can you come here for a moment," Leonardo calls from the front door a little before lunch. He stepped out earlier than normal today, heading into town before meeting with Augusto to discuss a trip to the realm with me. I want to pick up the little mementos I've managed to save over the years. Things that were my mother's, or of my time with her.

"Coming." I'm already turning the corner. In my hand, there's a glass of iced tea, which Isotta let me know he enjoys. I made it, too.

The way he looks at me as I reach him melts me on the spot. My core clenches at nothing but the memory of him in that shower a few days ago. We haven't done more than share a chaste kiss since then; a small pat on the ass or a hug every time we're near—they never last long enough—but that's as far as we've gone.

Something I'm both sad and thankful for. Because he listens to me, is aware of my nerves—but then leaves me wanting on the same breath.

Maybe I should tell him I want more?

There's no doubt in my mind he's mine, the man my mother told me would come and lay the world at my feet. The proof is in the sparks when we touch, the way his scent both calms and causes my heart to race—ignites my hunger for him.

He's all those things.

My savior. My weakness. Mine.

"There you are." *He's smiling, a cheeky grin that displays a dimple while he holds out a box toward me. It's from a brand I don't recognize, then again technology evades me, but I won't deny the giddy squeak I emit when I open it and a beautiful rose gold cell phone shines back at me. "This is so you always have a way to contact me, precious one. No matter where you are."*

I'm still not used to the device—not something allowed by our government—but I only have three numbers in my contacts list, which makes it easy to find him and then press green for dial.

It rings twice before I hear his labored breathing on the other end. "Hello, little mate. Miss me?" His playfulness brings a smile to my lips, but then the sound of a cackle interrupts what could've been a moment. My silence alerts him; Leonardo shouts to the trainers that he's leaving the sparring grounds and will be back later, as the wind around him rustles. As if he's running. "Is everything okay, Anaya?"

"You have visitors." Voice low. Subdued.

"Who?"

"The Rossi—"

He exhales through the line, relieved. "Babe, just tell Christopher to wait for me in my—"

"There's no Christopher here, Leonardo. Chiara's in the living room."

"The fuck." *My thoughts exactly.*

LEONARDO ENTERS the house exactly twenty minutes later, and his expression is nearly murderous. He only stops long enough to kiss me, grab my hand, and pull me with him into the sitting area.

That's where we find Isotta with a tray of drinks, the cup of tea beside their pops making me feel easier about this. Maybe I'm being petty, but just the sight of this woman makes me want to sit on his lap to prove a point. And as if he's reading my mind, my mate does just that.

There's a cuddler chair he ordered—one for every room—so that where he sat, I could be comfortable beside him. Always be with him.

Moreover, to annoy them, he waits until I'm settled before reaching for my porcelain flower cup.

"Oh!" the older woman, Lena, exclaims and pretends she is reaching for the same. "I thought that was for me. You don't mind, do you, Leo—"

"That's *Your Highness* or *King*, Miss Rossi. Do not confuse my graciousness with familiarity," he grits out, anger coming from him and spreading out into the room. Everyone bows but me; I'm getting better at not following the compulsions drilled into me since childhood. "And to answer your question, that tea is for my mate. If you desire one, it will be brewed, but not from this blend. This is hers."

"I see." Lena's face pinched tight, but she didn't say anything else on the matter.

"I'm glad that you do." After stirring the two cubes of sugar Isotta always adds for me, Leonardo makes it a point to bring the cup to my lips and waits until I sip and nod before placing it in my hands. "Now, what can I do for you?"

"Your Highness, I'm confused." Chiara's expression is perplexed. "You called for me to come. I thought—"

"I'm going to stop you right there." Lifting me, my mate carefully places me beside him before leaning forward. His jaw is tight, and his eyes are hard. "I never called *you*. My phone call was to Christopher Rossi, the leader of your coven, to come and meet with me today. *You* are not *him*."

Chiara's eyes well up with tears, her bottom lip trembling. "He hasn't been home in weeks. We don't know where he is."

"And yet you have his phone?"

"My king, Christopher left without a word to either of us. He left his clothes, car—everything belonging to him—we're at a loss."

"How long ago was this?"

"About a month, I'd say."

"Hmmm." Through the bond, I sense a mounting anger. The distrust he has for these two. "Why didn't you inform me of this last week? Why wait until now?"

"He's done this before. The anniversary—"

"Isotta, please escort them to guest house number three and make sure they're settled in before returning. They won't be leaving just yet."

"Yes, my king." Turning, she waves toward the door. "Please follow me."

"Leonardo, we don't need a guest house. I'm sure a room here would be—"

"Chiara, the guest house or a cell. Those are your choices."

"Thank you, Your Highness. We appreciate the accommodations." Lena stands, but I don't miss the subtle elbow jab to Chiara, nor the glare sent her way, a clear message to close her mouth. "We'll turn in for the day. Please let us know if you find anything."

Something tells me he won't, though. That he's gone.

"Are you ready?" Leonardo asks me early the next morning after I spent the night alone. The first one, but I understand the circumstances.

He's been holed up in his office since the Rossi family's arrival, sending out guards to their home and surrounding areas, but so far the two haven't located the elder. That's why not fifteen minutes ago, a tracker was dispatched and we found ourselves on the open training fields before the others were due to arrive for the first class of the day.

The area is large enough that they have a tactical obstacle, sparring section, and burn marked deep into the ground where young witches are tested.

This is also my first since arriving that I venture here. Nature is all around me. From the fresh scent of earth and large trees, to the damp soil with hints of moss and then a light, lingering breeze carrying fresh flowers, I'm in heaven.

It's been so long for me.

Taking in a deep breath, I let it out slowly while the part of me hidden from the world spreads. My wings flutter, their iridescent shimmer catching the early rays from the sun as I test their strength.

A bit tight from being unused, but strong. They flap twice, and the gust they create ruffles Leonardo's reddish hair. He scowls and pushes the longer strands back, but there's no missing the twitch in his lips.

"Brat."

"Maybe." A giggle slips through me. I'm positively giddy. "If I fall, I need you to promise you'll catch me. Don't let me crash and burn."

"Always."

"I'll hold you to that." Without further prompting, I unleash my inner fae and take off. The part of me that shares traits with humans has been at the forefront for so long, my powers and my desires hidden, so this is freeing.

And it comes to me as easy as breathing; I glide through trees with my fingers spread out, letting my fingertips caress each leaf. I swing through a small cropping of wildflowers near a lake, inhaling their sweet scent while the cooling mist coming off the water causes my skin to prickle with goosebumps.

I lost myself on this first flight in years. I've never been happier, and my mate is responsible. He's given me joy, security—and love— but more importantly, the time to discover each facet.

Most mates meet and mark within hours of meeting, but this thoughtful male is giving me experiences to build on. Like this one.

This is so special to me.

"Trusting you was the best choice—"

"Anaya!" It's a whisper but full of urgency, and I look down long enough to find a group of witches watching me. More than a few, actually, and it's my mate trying to get my attention.

He's waving his hand, almost commanding me to land, and I'm thrown off by the emotions coming through the bond once I focus.

Anger. Betrayal. Doubts.

"What the hell?" My landing is trickier than the takeoff and I fumble, nearly colliding with him. I expect him to catch me. For him to laugh at the clumsiness, but instead, his hands grip my shoulders to keep me at arm's length.

"Where are they?" It's a growl, spit out from between clenched teeth with a command infused through each word. "Where are Bruce and Ruben?"

CHAPTER 15
LEONARDO

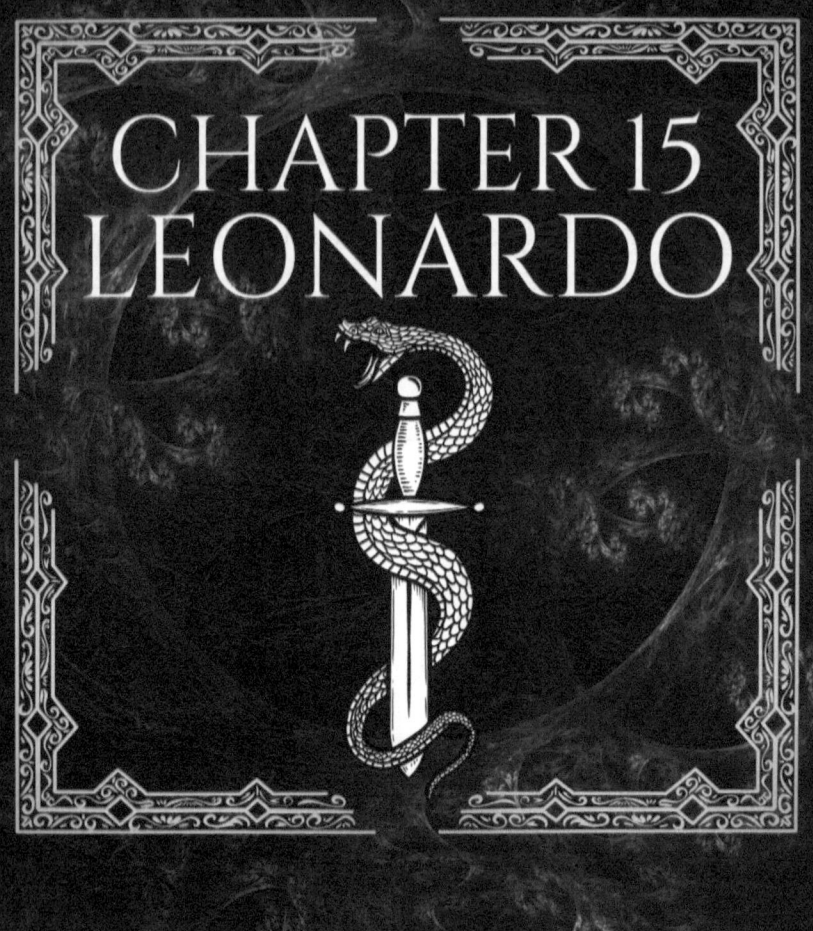

I 've been aware of Ruben and Brice's escape since a little after four a.m. by a night guard who'd found the door to their level unlocked and a trail of stench leading to the back exit. It stops there, just outside the rusted bars' threshold where it vanishes into thin air.

Only five people alive know about this passage, and four would never release those two monsters unless they wanted to play a hunting game with their spouses. This leads me to believe Silla has an ally in my coven, and they arrived yesterday.

The Rossi women aren't the brightest to show up declaring the coven's elder is missing, and while I search for the man, two under my nose vanish. It doesn't take a genius to add up this equation, but I'll play along for now.

I want Silla's head.

For my family. For Roberto, who's had his life stolen from him.

"Do you have any idea where she can be, Uncle?" The man tilts his head to the side, mulling, but then he begins to write furiously. If you looked at him both now and the day Anaya saved him, it's like looking at two different people. He's less skittish, and although the reintegration into our Wiccan society has been slow, I see the improvement. He seeks out certain members; Augusto and Anaya are two of those people.

The first is because they're life-long friends: guilt that Augusto— we—are all dealing with.

The latter, because she knows a part of his life no one else does: Anaya has his complete trust.

Turning the notebook in my direction, he shows me our first real clue.

Marsilla is now the sole owner of a property in Neuilly.
The building is one of the most expensive in the area and only she occupies it.
She's minutes from Paris, Leonardo.
Hiding in plain sight.

"Are you sure? Do you have an address?"

Not exactly, but I remember the name of a women's boutique on a bag the last time she came to see me.

*She'd come in to share some good news. Marsilla
wanted to come home.*

"When was this? Home?" I ask, my jaw ticking. "This is not her home. She's not—"

Uncle Roberto holds up one hand while writing with the other. It's sloppier than the last note, but his emotions are raw. Angry. A bit bitter, and he's within his rights to be so.

*I'd rather kill myself than allow her to further taint
my brother's legacy.
I should've done a better job of protecting you three,
but I'll never make the same mistake again. My mate
will die for what she's done.*

"I'm sorry, Uncle. We failed you, too." It's a shame I'll carry for the rest of my life. How we didn't do more to find him—force him to give us an explanation of what occurred that day. Maybe if we'd looked, this man could've come home and lived his life in peace—escaped that nightmare.

*You were a kid, Leo. A babe.
You'd just lost your parents while trying to navigate the
responsibilities placed on your head—to protect these
lands at all costs. You watched a woman come in and
hurt your aunt, whom you loved, and then drag me
through a portal without my putting up much of a
fight. Yes, I was glamoured, but how were you
supposed to know that?
What could you have done?*

"I'm not a kid anymore. This time I'm not lying down or waiting for an attack."

Then prepare for war now, and not the day it arrives at your doorstep.
She's more vicious than her brother and plays the long game, Leo. She's been dropping clues along the way as a warning. Don't get me wrong—in a sick way, she cares about you, always has, but that won't stop her from coming after what you love.
Protect Anaya at all costs.

IF HEARTBREAK HAD AN EXPRESSION, this would be it. Anaya doesn't know how to answer me or what to do with herself—her end of the bond is screeching at me that she's scared—yet my worry overrides any logic at the moment. How those two assholes escaped eludes me, and being played for a fool doesn't sit well with me.

Someone betrayed me. A member of my coven will die before the day is through.

"Where would they go, Anaya?"

"You don't trust me?" Small. Hurt. Those four words are heavy with sadness. Tears pool in her eyes, and the sight cuts me deep; I'm going to repay the traitor's kindness with a dose of my own. With me, she's supposed to be safe at all times and living freely—never in fear. It's unacceptable, but what's worse, it's like reliving my parents' last days all over again.

The knowledge that someone you trusted betrayed you...

That they'd hurt someone you love for selfish gain...

Because I do. Since that first day, this slip of a girl has owned my heart, and I don't want it back. Not now. Not ever.

My feelings for her have grown, even if I owe her more than pretty words. I owe her romance, something I'll be remedying tonight. At the very least, we'll take a step in the right direction.

"Precious one, look at me." I'm swallowing hard, feeling her slip through my fingers. She's putting up a wall, yet our bond is unforgiving. Without marking each other, I'm attuned to every single part of her. Which gives me an idea. *If you can hear me, look up.*

The quickness in which her head snaps up gives me relief, which she feels on her end, and her brows furrow. Confusion settles onto her face. "How are—"

"Do you know where they are? Answer me, Anaya." *Play along, precious one. We have a traitor, and I'll explain later.* "What allies do they have near here?"

The mounting tension drops from her end now, almost instantaneously, but the tears from earlier still fall. The drops had gathered and grown, and now play perfectly into the moment.

"I don't know, Leonardo. Please believe me." The hands at her sides are shaking, her wings dulling a bit from their luminescent splendor, and I curse those who ruined this moment for her. She was so excited today when I offered the area for her to test out their strength—her muscles—after days of being lethargic. Curing Roberto took a bigger toll on her than she first believed. "How could this happen? They're going to come for me."

"Or did you let them out?" The moment the question leaves me, shocked gasps surround us, and I'm happy to hear so many of the females she's befriended hiss on her behalf. *They love you, Anaya. Just like I can't live without you. I trust you.* "Where were you last night while I was in my office? Did you sneak out to help your brother and his general?"

"No! I swear I didn't!" *Can you hear me?* Her sweet voice inside my head is a blessing and calms me down so that I don't act without proof. Because I'm no longer an idiot; I learned my lessons on coincidences the day I found my beautiful little fae. And like that day, I want to bathe the world in my enemy's blood.

I'd burn the world to the ground, as long as she's safe.

There's no limit on what I'd do for her.

I hear you. Your voice is adorable, baby. So sweet.

It doesn't hurt with you. Why is that?

"That's enough, Brother." Right on cue, Gabriella steps through those gathered and places herself between us, Anaya behind her. Her stance is protective, and for further proof, she extends a hand back, which my mate grabs onto. *You are going to go with her, Anaya. I'll be with you soon.* "You're accusing your mate of treason. Those are high charges, and until you have proof, I'm taking Aya with me."

"She's not leaving."

"Yes. I am." Turning to look at my sister, Anaya gives her a small smile. "Please get me out of here."

As we agreed on the phone, Gabriella turns and walks away with Anaya while Theodore watches their backs. They'd gone home a few days ago but came back at my request to play this role. Their guards are with them, too, and Tero gives me a subtle nod of the head in snake form when they make it to a portal at the opposite end of the field.

They step through without issue, my sister hugging Anaya, but before she goes, I hear her one last time in my head:

When you're connected with me through our private link, it's like a pleasurable caress to my senses, Leonardo. It fills me with warmth, whereas my father used our mental link as his favorite form of punishment. Thank you for showing me the difference, my king. I'll be waiting for you.

147

CHAPTER 16
Anaya

"**A**re you sure no one here will hate me?" I ask Gabriella, a slight tremble in my voice as we exit their private jet a short ride later. This is the second time I've been on a plane, although for the first, I wasn't lucid. I'd slept from Canada to Italy while Leonardo held me close, never straying far from me.

And even while asleep, a part of me was aware of this.

I heard his low words. He wasn't speaking to me, but I felt them just the same.

Love is the most powerful thing in the world, Leo. No matter the species or your beliefs, we are all worthy of unconditional love, son.

So when you find her, cherish your mate. Honor her and your bond, even if at times this brings you pain.

Is that what he meant? The being in pain?

Because since the moment I walked away from him, hearing his words of encouragement and promising me it would be okay, I've felt empty. This is worse than going through the pains of what I thought was rejection, because now I know what waking beside your mate feels like. The butterflies I get by saying his name—the look of pride on his face when he sees me experience something for the first time.

Like the day I discovered my love for smiley stickers and colorful highlighters. It might not seem important to some, but they're pretty and I like to leave him a *Have A Good Day* on his bedside table every morning before he leaves for the training grounds or his office.

The first time I made a cookie, he ate it like it was a decadent pastry. Didn't care that the bottom was burned to a crisp and probably tasted like soot.

That's love.

And I love him.

I should've told him before I left.

"You are safe, Anaya," Gabriella says, pulling me from those sad thoughts. I need to trust that this separation is to keep me safe. "No one in our kingdom would dare lay a hand on you."

"Thank you."

"Family takes care of one another. Never thank us for that."

"Mine causes pain." The words slip before I have a chance to rein them in. They cause the vampire king to snap his head in our direction. He pauses at the now-open doorway of the plane and meets my eyes. There's no coldness in the red; if anything, I find warmth. *Just like with Xadiel.* "I'm sorry. That just—"

"I'd ask my father to give Larue his life again, just to slice his head off myself. Although, I think Leo might fight me for the honor.

That bastard was an animal, Anaya, and even they protect their offspring."

"He's right, you know." Gabby bumps her shoulder with mine before exiting the plane. They wait for me at the bottom of the short stairs, the long coral-colored summer dress I'm wearing fluttering in the strong breeze coming from the ocean mere steps away. The runway is on a cliff adjacent to the vampiric castle, but that's not what has my attention.

Mere feet from me is a man in a mid-shift change. His body has white scales, eyes a near milk-like sky blue, and his head snaps in my direction once my feet reach the tarmac. I'd seen him back in the field, but the man did not travel with us on the plane.

I'm staring. I know I am.

I've never encountered other species before, and in the last few weeks, I've surrounded myself with the top of each food chain from these three kingdoms.

"Welcome home, Your Majesties." The words come out in a low hiss, exaggerating each ending syllable. I saw glimpses of him during the confrontation with my father, standing at the end of the stairs—he guarded my back until we boarded the plane—and now here. "How was your flight?"

While his tone is friendly, I get the impression the question is about me. My mental state.

"She's fine, old friend. Anaya's a strong one."

"Of that, we have no doubt. May I?" Theodore and Gabriella give him a nod, and he walks over slowly. The gait of a predator, yet the closer he gets, I can't help but smile. In his eyes, I see a friend. In his aura, I read loyalty. "I'm Tero, Miss Anaya. Welcome to our home, although I have a feeling you won't be here for long."

"Thank you, but why is that?" I ask, raising a brow in surprise. How sure he is of this.

"Because your mate has called me twenty times, young one. He cannot stay away."

"TERO WAS WRONG."

It's been three days since I arrived here and I've yet to receive a call or text, something his sister has been teaching me to do. We've grown close, the three of us, and while Isabella isn't here in person—she's still feeling the "after" effects of her heat—we video chat and catch up every day.

This is what having siblings is supposed to be like.

We talk, and they help me deal with the separation that slowly eats at me more and more every day. I miss him. I want Leonardo, but I've kept my word and I'm waiting for him to fulfill his promise and come for me.

I've told his sister this, and they're wonderful about keeping me occupied. Gabriella is obsessed with helping me learn to dress for my age and as a queen, while Isabella gives the advice a mother would.

"Did the new box of clothes come in yet?" Isa asks by way of a greeting. She's dressed in her signature white, this time an overall and a fitted, plain top combo—her hair up high in a ponytail. I didn't accept the call, but with her, it doesn't matter. My phone just answers. "I sent you a few things from one of the boutiques here, Aya. The she-wolf who owns it designs the prettiest dresses."

"Just did, Isa," I say, smiling at how right the family-only nick-name feels—how it further proves that I belong with them. *Owned by her brother.* "But this isn't a few items. You sent me the full store."

"Shut it, you. Open it."

"Give me a sec…" Shifting to find some sort of sharp object to use, but come up empty. I'm on the floor below the king and queen, a suite meant for family or important guests, and it has everything. There hasn't been a single item I searched for and couldn't find. *So where are the scissors?*

"Last drawer on the right, and surprise!"

"That's cheating." But she's right, and after finding a pair of scissors, I cut across the tape. Yet that's as far as I get; her face on the screen is frozen at an awkward picture. She looks afraid.

A second later, all the lights go out in the room, and the call drops while a hand is placed over my eyes. My initial reaction is to bite or scream, my fangs dropping a little lower than usual, but then his scent hits me. *Leonardo.*

"I should be mad at you." Breathless. Excited. Whole.

Those three words describe me to a T, but they fall flat once I'm whirled around and our eyes meet again. It's like the first time all over again—the second our eyes met and my world righted itself. All I see and feel is him—my mate.

"Hello, little mate."

"Hello, my king." My arms find their place around his neck, tugging him close until not a breath separates us. And he reciprocates, wrapping me in his strong arms while meeting me halfway for a too-short, yet sweet kiss. Leonardo nuzzles me, his lips skimming across my cheeks then chin then back to my lips before dotting each I.

I'm home.

"I've missed you."

"As I you."

"Ready to get out of here for a bit?"

"Really?" Won't deny I'm excited to spend time with him in any way I can. "Where are we going?"

"It's a surprise."

LEONARDO

As you grow up, I want you to remember the lessons I've taught you. Never forget that volatile emotions are uncontrollable and will kill you from within. That you must always be fair and just, and lead our people without prejudice over what's happened here today— don't place the blame on an innocent's head because of mere association. Not everything is as it seems.

Words I've been repeating in my head for the last hour as I make my way to my mate. We've been without the other for days— hundreds of miles apart—yet her end of the binds sings for me. It's inside my chest and alive, always present, and when I close my eyes at night, it's a small light that pulses with one of my heartbeats.

Not diminished, but stronger. So precious to me, and I understand my father's words now more than ever. Being without her is torture, and I couldn't wait any longer.

So, I had a little help from my sister who created a private dinner for us out on one of the upper-level balconies. It'll be away from everyone, just the two of us, and exactly what I need after spending the last few days tracking Chiara and Lena through Paris.

Because they'd been Silla's accomplices, but the building Uncle Roberto mentioned was empty and deserted. The ones nearby are occupied by people who work, own a business nearby, or commute to Paris on the regular. If she's hiding in plain sight, it's not in Neuilly.

Close? Yes.

I've caught her scent a few times, a trail that's maybe a week or two old, but in the end, I'm back to square one. *It's only a matter of time, though.* Knowing Roberto is safe and under our protection has to be pissing her off. She'll make a mistake.

"Are you ready, love?"

"I am." Leading her out the door, I find the castle empty outside of guards, and they remain in the lower levels. They make the rounds and give me a nod in passing, while I ascend past the second left and then another set of stairs. This one leads to an area of the castle where no one is allowed without the king's approval.

There's an old Victorian key that opens the gated door and I hand it to Anaya, who grins at me. That tug inside my chest is a happy one. She's almost jumping from the excitement, opening the creaking door and stepping through as I turn on the sconces that lead the way.

There's only one room here; Gabriella claims it as her meditation room, but what we walk into is more than just a cozy dinner set for two. This is perfection; I'd brought things from home to help set it up and explained what I wanted, but that's as far as the woman let me help.

My sister did this for us, and I can't thank her enough for it. The look in Anaya's eyes, the way her perfect lips part into an O shape as she takes everything in, is one I will tuck away and hold onto for the rest of my days.

She's glowing. Her beautiful blue aura expands as tears form in her eyes.

Those violet eyes sweep across the room once—three times— memorizing the most minute detail. She takes the room in fully, from the Parisian rug to the cozy table set for two with golden goblets and a meal beneath round domes that I cooked in their kitchen.

Nothing too fancy, but I know she enjoys the food of my country. The pasta dish I made for her Isotta taught me to make—pancetta is the star accompanied by a cream reduction and a few peas to add a touch of sweetness. There's bread and wine, and for dessert, I baked a two-layer chocolate cake because that's what I smell like to her.

"I love it, Leonardo. Thank you." A breeze sweeps in and shifts the linens on the table, causing Anaya to close her eyes for a second with a contented smile. She stays like that for a second or two before righting them, and I pour us each a glass of wine. This one is a bit more on the sweet side than I would normally drink, but the way she licks her lips after the first few sips makes it an automatic favorite of mine. More so when she leans over and places her lips on mine in a chaste kiss. "This is perfection."

"I'd do anything for you, Anaya Larue." My heart races inside my chest as I take her hand in mine, and she picks up on my nerves. On the way my end of the bond vibrates.

"You okay?"

"I am, just have a lot to say. To explain to you."

"Don't be? It's just us." A cheeky wink from her breaks the tension on my end, pulling a deep chuckle from me. Anaya calms me. "Besides, this is my first official date, and it's already everything I'd ever wished it to be."

"Is that so? How about if I do this?" Placing my glass down, I use my grip on her hand to tug her against my chest. She stumbles a bit from the sudden move but laughs while placing her other hand on my chest, right over my heart. Automatically, my lips seek out hers, and this kiss is everything I've missed about us.

It's soft and sweet, but then she moans, and I take it without pause. My mouth plunders hers, reacquainting myself with her taste —the feel of her curves against my much harder planes. I seek her little whines between nibbles. I touch and caress every single inch of her within reach as the priceless possession she is.

Mine. Always.

I slow our kisses down to a few sweeps across her lips. Calm my breathing down, and then speak against her lips, "I accept you as you are, Anaya. The good, the bad, and every moment that you gift me in between. I'm going to take care of you, precious one. Always."

"I love you, too, Leonardo. Always."

We stay like that for a few minutes, just hugging and enjoying the moment, but then she grimaces. It's followed by a cough, and she steps out of my embrace while her eyes turn red and she points to her throat.

Anaya's breathing becomes labored rapidly, and I lay her down on the ground before pulling out my phone and sending my sister a quick message. Once it goes through, I toss the device aside and lower my mouth to hers, ready to start giving her CPR—aid her lungs get air in—when I see it. Nestled on the side of her head is a long, thin dart that I pull out and bring to my nose, sniffing it. My eyes widen when I realize it's made out of solid iron with a salt-like substance dripping from its tip to add to the pain; to burn her from within.

There's also an engraving at the end; the name *Prince Ruben* spelled out neatly.

Motherfuck. How the hell did—

"Leonardo…it's iron." She's gasping, the pretty color of her cheeks turning pallid while the area around where the dart pricked becomes deathly grey. Her veins bulge, pushing against her skin.

"Slow breaths, baby. Keep them slow and steady…like that." My finger is on her pulse, and it's low. Her chest has trouble rising. She's weakening too fast from the poison. "Follow my lead, precious… that's it." My phone chimes then. I'm sure it's Gabriella, but I don't look away from Anaya to check. This can't be happening. I cannot lose her. "Good girl. We're going to get you help."

"I'm okay." A wheeze. Choking, then a splutter of blood that stains her pretty dress while a few drops land on my cheek. Slipping a hand beneath her back, I gently pull her to me and use my body heat to help warm her as tears pool in my eyes. They fall into her hair, the blonde locks so long and soft. "Healing myself, but it's going to be slow. Hurts."

"Don't exert yourself." *Gods, don't take her from me. Please.* "Just stay relaxed and breathe with me."

It took me a hundred and thirteen years to find the love of my life.

It took him a mere second to almost end her.

Yet the stupidest mistake a man like him could make is showing his face as I hold Anaya close and tears fall from my eyes.

"I told you once that a snake in the grass always has friends. Do you remember that?" Ruben lands on the open balcony then and my head snaps up, watching as he stretches his wings. They're ugly and misshapen, the dark feathers molting with each movement he makes. The man is also smart enough not to cross the threshold. "You didn't mow your lawn, Leonardo."

"You're a sick fuck like your father, Larue. I'm going to kill you."

"Big words from a man about to lose it all." His eyes sweep

across my gift for his sister and a sneer overtakes his face, his expression one of disgust. Ruben kicks a small table beside the chaise lounge; it tips over, sending the vase brimming with pink roses and a chilled bottle of champagne to the ground. They crash and shatter upon impact, a thousand small shards ruining our after-dinner surprise; I wanted to watch the stars with her. To cuddle her under a blanket and talk about everything and nothing, to just enjoy being in her presence.

But he took that from us.

"You hurt your sister." That same rush of dark magic I felt on the day of my parents persecution thrashes within my veins. It's a part of me I've kept hidden all these years, focusing instead on the lessons taught by my parents and not the calling for blood—destruction—I'm yearning for. I've tried. I've fought. *No more.* "You tried to kill my heart."

"Sentimental attachments are for the weak, *Your Highness*." Venom drips from the formal address while glass crunches under his shoes. He lowers himself into a squat; I'm not an idiot. The pussy is preparing himself to fly off just in case. "That's why I love nothing. No one."

"She's your family, asshole. How could you hurt family?" Outside, the sky darkens and the winds pick up, a bolt of lightning crashing to the ground just beyond the balcony. "That was your second biggest mistake."

"And the first?" Condescending. Goading.

"Showing your face."

There's nothing more rabid than a man about to lose it all.

I am that beast.

Because the second the door burst open and my sister rushed in frantically yelling, I gave chase.

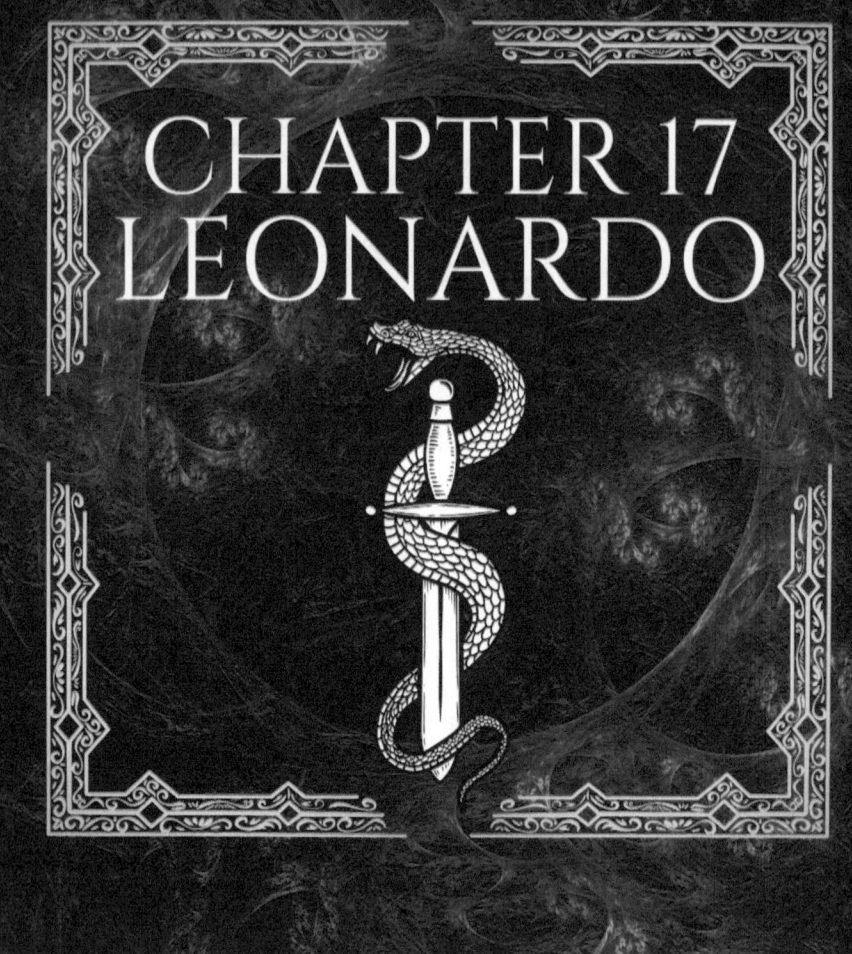

CHAPTER 17
LEONARDO

Ruben recoils when he sees my sister and her mate, the guards poised to strike behind them, but I hold a single hand out toward them. They will not touch him. He's my prey.

Thunder rolls through the sky, the sound loud and ominous before a bolt strikes the ocean not far from here. That strike settles something in me, and I look down at the woman who owns my heart for a second, taking in her beautiful face. From her closed eyes to her cheeks—the fullness of her perfectly pink lips—she is mine. Made for me by the gods to awaken the part of my soul I thought died along with my parents.

Those scars are still fresh, they hurt, but losing the woman in my arms would kill me.

She is what true love is. The very definition of the words.

"Take care of her, Gabriella." My voice is hoarse but the command is clear, and my family doesn't take offense. If anything, they understand that right now, I am not her brother but a man who has had enough—this is my rock bottom—and I am taking my pound of flesh.

Gently, I lay her down before kissing Anaya on the lips. "I'll be right back, my love. Wait for me." For a few seconds, I get no response. A wheezing sound leaves her throat with every exhale while tears fall from the corners of her closed eyes, but then there's a tiny squeeze of my hand. It's minute, so soft, as is the word *always* that accompanies it a second later. "I love you, Anaya. Forgive me for what I must do."

"We have her, Leo," Theodore says and I nod.

Because I trust them. Because I feel their anger—it merges with my own—and I exhale roughly before standing and then tilting my head in their direction. My cold eyes remain on him, though. On the soon-to-be-dead prince of the fae court. "Iron in her system. Get a healer."

Ruben inches back; he's stupid for not leaving sooner. He's gauging reactions, not taking into account the danger he's in. Any one of us could kill him, but idiocy keeps him there. Enjoying his handiwork.

"I will not let her die, Brother. End him and make it painful."

"He will not live to see the moon rise," I vow, and that's when he takes a step back, then another. Ruben's edging himself to the railing and when I take my first step toward him, he dives back and I follow.

I throw myself over the railing of the balcony after him.

His flying isn't graceful like Anaya's who soared through the open field and trees as if she were dancing while letting the wind guide each delicate, yet sensual movement. No. This is clumsy, and I wonder how Ruben managed to get up so high if he struggled to maintain momentum.

Because his abilities remind me more of a bird taking flight for the first time, rather than such an old fae like himself.

The area below the balcony is a garden with sunflowers, and we're coming close to it. Their yellow color is bright, and I watch them sway in a small breeze as Ruben manages to catch a little propulsion at the last moment, his eyes on the upcoming ground below while rising a few feet back up and in my direction.

In all this, he didn't look back.

He's within my grasp, and I fist his head while using my downward drive to slam us right onto the ground. We land with a harsh thump, his body taking the brunt of the crash, and I smile when a section of his right wing snaps, hanging limp.

Ruben screams while guards standing by surround us—not getting involved, but so that he doesn't attempt to take flight once more. Not that it worries me; I'd catch him before the man reached any height.

"I curse the bitch," he spits, attempting to push me off but I don't move. Ruben's smaller, weaker, and a total disgrace of a man. He's spent his life being a lapdog for their deceased father, not accomplishing anything on his own. For himself. "Father should've drowned them the day Amelia tried to escape with Anaya."

"Fuck did you say?" I snarl, lifting his head and then slamming it back against the compacted ground. There are a few large rocks beneath us. They've been unearthed by our crash, rough and with a few sharp corners, the biggest connecting with the back of his skull. A cut appears and blood rises, spilling from the wound no larger than a coin. "He killed her mother?"

"He couldn't." A groan follows that turns into a hacking laugh; his pitch similar to that of a hyena. "If she dies, the real heir will step into her powers. The crown isn't handed over in the physical sense but manifests, and all faes would drop to their knees before Anaya. She would take what's mine."

"You're the older sibling."

"That cunt is not my sister." That earns him an elbow to the face, then another. I will not accept any form of disrespect from him or anyone else when it comes to her. "Please stop."

"Then watch yourself, Ruben. Choose your words carefully."

"Understood." He shifts uncomfortably, tries to throw a punch at my face, and fails terribly. There's no real strength in his arms, it's almost like fighting an untrained child. Young witches in my coven have better defensive instincts than him. "Understood."

"Then finish."

"She doesn't deserve the crown." Blue-tinged blood pools in his mouth and Ruben tries to turn his face and spit it out, but I shake my head. I force him to swallow it down with nothing more than the narrowing of my eyes. He gags, and I raise a brow—wave an impatient hand for him to continue. "It's mine. My kingdom. I've worked too hard to back away now."

"Why does she think you're her kin?" At first, the prince doesn't answer. He's testing my patience again, yet the second I raise my arm to clock him, he begins to mumble. Low. Indiscernible. "Louder, asshole. Why does my female think you're related?"

"Father killed my mother after the whore birthed me." There's a small lisp now, the torn flesh of his upper lip and what looks like a dislocated jaw causing this. I do enjoy the way he grimaces the more he talks. "He couldn't to have a mistress ruin his glamor on Amelia."

"And where's Amelia now?" I ask instead of telling the dumb fuck he'll never get close to becoming king. He's lucky if he sees the next hour, much less wears a crown. "Where did Larue hide her?"

"I'd never tell you. They both got what they deserve."

"Last chance, asshole. Tell me."

"Fuck. You." My next blow comes from above him; I mount his midsection and pick up the jagged rock that caused the gash before bringing it down against his nose. Once. Twice. Five times, and the area is nearly black when I pull back, his blue-tinged blood soaking us both. He's cut once again across the bridge of his nose, but this time it extends to his cheeks. "Stop!"

"No." Two quick strikes to the affected area have him thrashing beneath me, trying to buck me off, but I have a part of his wing pinned beneath my knee. "Theodore should've ripped these from your body instead of clipping them. You don't deserve them."

"Get off, you son of...fuck!" Dropping the rock, I pull out my favorite dagger and flick it open before stabbing the area closest to where they protrude from his back. I hit the bone but force the sharp steel through before twisting my hand. And much like brittle bone, after some pressure, it shatters. "No! Don't...please."

Now I get his fear.

I want more. Need it.

The second wing goes much the same, and I'm almost too caught up by the thirst in me for vengeance to catch his next low words as I sever it. "I'm not her only enemy, Leonardo. Kill me, and another will come for her."

Wearing his blood and chest heaving, I stare him down. "What does that mean?"

"Ask Gabriella about the name Veltross."

"I know who they are, and that bloodline is dead."

Ruben is ashen and weak from his sanguine loss, the steady drip from the torn wings and wounds to his head saturating the ground. Vampires hiss around me. They sound angry, and it's either from the dirty blood or the name of their general from a century ago.

The same man who killed their queen. Who took my sister away from us for just as long.

"No. It's not." He coughs, and that's when I notice the way I'm pressing the dagger against his neck, I've cut through the dermis already. "One more."

"Who?" I growl out, slicing a little deeper. "Give me their name."

"I'll never tell you that." A whisper; he's losing consciousness.

"But did you know there's a tracker implemented in Anaya's right shoulder blade? It's how I found her. How others will, too."

That last bit of information, the level of violation against my female by the same people who were supposed to protect her, throws me over the edge. I wield the dagger as if it were a sword and drive it through his neck, pushing with my weight until I meet bone and even that doesn't stop me. And that power I've been pushing back aids me now. Electricity sparks and my hands control each volt; I use the metal of the blade to conduct it, burning Ruben where his flesh meets the weapon, and then beyond.

Once again, the sky cracks, but this time its charge finds me.

Enhances and booms and the fiery lash strikes him from different angles. The scent of burned flesh mixes in the air and swirls around while his last breaths stutter. Choke. Ruben tries to scream, but there's no way for him to do so as I've severed him from skin to windpipe and then vertebrae.

He's dying, and I stay right as I am until he is no more.

Only then do I pull back and the dark skies ease, slowly revealing a setting sun on the horizon.

"Your Majesty," Tero says then, and I turn my head in his direction. I don't remember his arrival, but the look of pride on his face almost makes me smile. Almost, because without my precious mate, there is no joy or meaning.

"Yes, Tero?"

"Miss Anaya's awake and needs you."

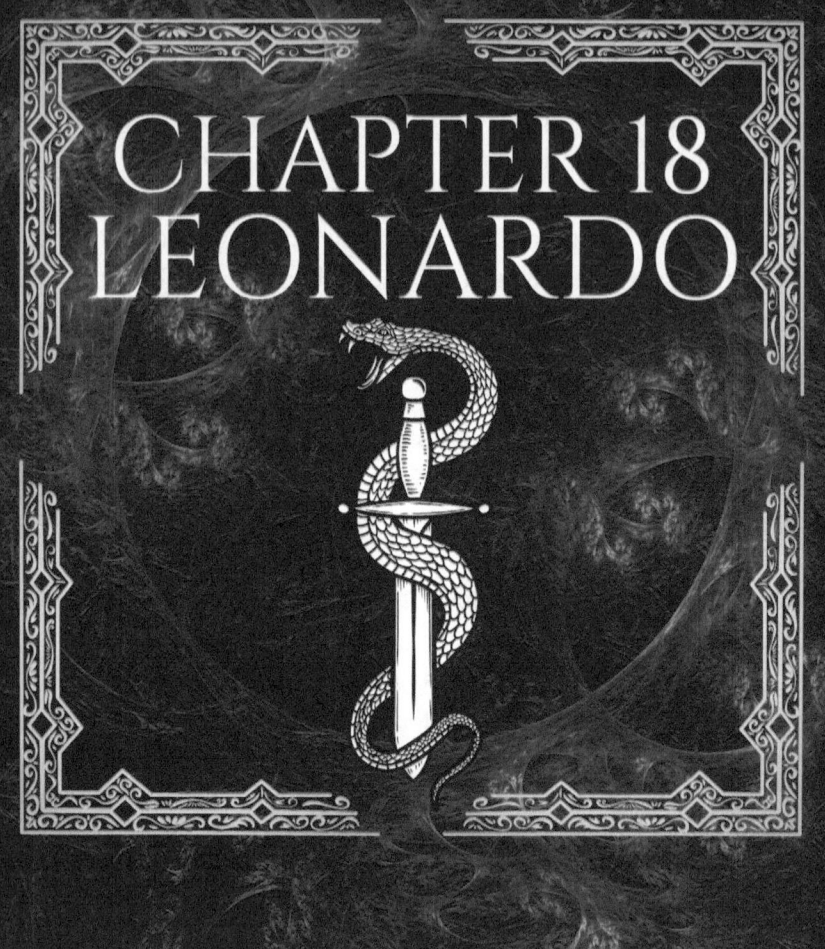

CHAPTER 18
LEONARDO

Anaya's lying on a bed of white linens and soft pillows when I step inside the room she's been occupying. She's pale, but her breathing is calmer than when I left, and it's thanks to the woman giving me a small smile beside her mate.

It's just the two of them inside, and upon my return, Theo moves to stride past me but then stops. He places a hand on my arm. "I'm sorry, Leo. She was under my care, and I let you down. I will bring you the head of those responsible for aiding Ruben."

While I appreciate the sentiment, he's wrong. Her care and protection are my main priorities, and I failed to do both.

"It's not on you. I'm her mate." Theodore's not offended by my words. If anything, he understands how I feel more than anyone at the moment. "But I do need a favor."

"Anything."

"Find the last surviving Veltross member and bring them to me."

"How do you know? I've been searching—"

"Ruben was a very chatty man."

I don't need to say anything else, and he doesn't ask. My brother-in-law simply nods and then leaves, closing the door behind him while I take in my mate's beauty.

Delicate and tempting, Anaya looks like a living doll as she lies there perfectly still. There's a sheet covering her from view, but her bare shoulders and lack of bra strap tell me she's naked underneath, something also highlighted by the tightening of her nipples under my heated gaze a few seconds later.

Our bond hasn't weakened. If anything, it's stronger than when I left her. It sings for me in the sweetest *hello* while my side responds with an *I need you.*

"The iron is slowly leaving her system," Gabriella says, pulling my attention away from my female for a second. Just enough to meet her eyes, nod, and then I'm back to watching Anaya. Needing. Cataloging.

The more natural, rhythmic rise and fall of her chest, how tiny she is—how her lips quirk up just a little because she knows I'm watching.

Can you hear me, precious one?

I don't get a verbal response, but there's an affirmative hum back.

A low noise she made from the back of her throat, but it is enough for me. Let's me know she's aware, here with me, and going to be okay.

I love you, Anaya. Always will.

This earns me a stronger noise, more like the girlish squeak she makes when happy.

Think you can open your eyes for me?

"Whatever you're doing, keep it up. I feel her getting stronger."

"That's because she's my little fighter. Always so brave."

Gabriella places a hand over Anaya's chest. Checking her over. "Aya's a powerful healer, Leo. She literally beat me to the punch. I've barely had to manipulate her tethers…"

"Why the trail off?"

"Isabella told me this would happen. She called before you texted to warn us, and then again after you ran off. Both times she promised all Anaya needed to pull through was to feel secure. Accepted."

That makes me feel better. It also cements what will happen next.

"Thank you, Sister. I appreciate your help."

"Of course. That's what—" Understanding dawns on her. "You want me to leave and clear the floor?"

"I'd appreciate that."

With a knowing grin on her face, Gabriella exits, but not before giving me a quick hug. And no sooner does she close the door, this side of the castle empties of all beings. I hear the retreating footsteps of guards rushing away, and the only sound that now accompanies me is the steady heartbeat of my female.

I'm focused on its cadence. The thump, thump, thump is the prettiest little sound, and I let it pull me toward her. Guide me, until I'm at the foot of her bed.

She will be my first and last, my only, and I follow the call of our bond. Because instinct is a wondrous thing; I know what she needs.

It's there in the link that connects us. Moreover, nothing will solidify her side of our unity like my wearing her bite. The perfect indent of her teeth, the fangs she tries to hide but I've seen. I noticed her shyness over them the first time they dropped.

Unconsciously inside the shower, they peeked at me and I found them beautiful. Wanted to lick their tiny points, but she closed her eyes and gave me a closed-lip smile.

She was tired still and I let it go, the healing of my uncle taking a lot out of her, but her grins were never as free…

Until the day she took flight on Wiccan land. Whether it was endorphins or losing the rigid grip she keeps on her behavior, Anaya let go. Giggled and laughed until I had to pretend to blame her for something she didn't do.

The guilt over that situation will forever haunt me because he poisoned her. Almost took her from me. *Yet we now know her mother is alive.*

News that will both hurt and bring her joy.

Mate. Need mate.

"I'm here, precious one." Stripping out of my clothes, I kick the soiled shirt and trousers toward the bathroom where they land near the sink. I'm not allowing his traitorous stench to ruin this moment, yet I also don't make a move to clean off his blood. Contradictory, I know, but these are my warrior markings, the proof that he will never reach her again. The promise that I will kill for her every time if need be.

And the day I find Brice and Silla, I'll do the same.

Need mate. Close. Bite.

"I'll wear it with pride, too." Anaya's shifting beneath the soft, white sheet. Her body undulates and arches, thighs spreading the closer I get, causing the fabric to fall beneath her breasts. They're bigger than a handful and perky, the dusty pink nipples tight and waiting for my touch. I climb over her, and the mattress dips from our combined weight. She's hot, her heat and scent enveloping me in a blanket of lust as I hover over her covered cunt. "Nothing would make me happier, Aya."

Strawberries and cream; I taste her in the air between my mouth and her pussy. She's so sweet and mouthwatering; I almost bury my face between her thighs. Lose myself in Anaya's slick warmth, but instead, I pause.

I want to take my time with her. No rush.

Because there will never be a second of our union where I don't worship every single inch of her. For the rest of our lives, it will be my honor to do so every morning and night.

Laying a kiss at the top of her mound earns me a keening sound.

So pretty.

Please, mate. Bite. Love.

Her voice in my head is stronger now, sultry, and I reward her by sliding the sheet off and then dragging my teeth from her pelvis to her breasts. From right to left, I trail them over her lightly sweaty skin, leaving light red welts on her fair skin before taking a tight peak between my blunt teeth.

I can't bite her the way she'll do me, but I will make her feel them.

At the first nip, she arches and hums once more. This time vocally. It's all the encouragement I need, and I do it again, rougher this time, before laving the beaded nipple with my tongue. I flick—lick—it a few times before suckling hard and pulling more of her breast into my mouth before switching to the other.

And while I do, her body tries to fight my hold.

Her eyes are closed, but she's aware of my every move. Arching up in offering and I accept, taking hold of her other tit and squeezing the supple flesh. Bounce it a bit to test the weight in my palm while I pull her nipple with each suction—drag my teeth over the puckered skin before switching breasts.

I repeat the same torture until she kicks off more of the sheet with her movements, and it's like watching a present unwrap itself. The blanket stops at her hips, and I can tell it bothers her, but I don't help. Instead, I follow its trajectory down and after tweaking a nipple with the tip of two fingers, I kiss down her abdomen from her ribs to her belly button, and then stop an inch above where the fabric ends.

"Motherfuck, baby. You smell so good."

Leonardo, please.

"What do you need, my precious one? Tell me with your lips and I'll reward you."

"You." One word, and it's muffled. And had I not been so attuned to her; I would've missed it. Yet I heard, and the sound to me is beautiful.

"Good girl." With one hand, I yank the offending sheet off and toss it to the floor while I lean down and nuzzle the soft strip of hair there. She's bare everywhere else and her clit is swollen, dripping with her arousal that leaves a shiny coat on her pink flesh. My mouth waters at the sight, the ravenous hunger leading me to my meal by an invisible leash, and I growl as the first taste of her slick bathes my tongue. Tangy and sweet and mine; I cannot control myself and fist my cock with one hand while I force her thighs apart with my shoulders. They're broad and spread her wide, almost obscenely so, and yet it's not enough.

I lick her from her entrance to clit and then swirl my tongue over the swollen bundle of nerves. It throbs, pulsing as I flatten my tongue and drag it a few times over it. Then lower and I'm dipping into her tiny hole, pushing against the wave of her body clenching in need.

I'm sucking her juices, rubbing my mouth over every inch of her cunt, but then my hair is yanked and my eyes snap up to hers. I don't take my mouth off her pussy, though, or stop stroking my cock, a sight that has her panting hard. Those violet eyes of hers storm and the fangs I've longed to feel drop, her top lip curling back so I see them.

Her. Just like this.

Wanton and free and mine.

My mouth curls against her slick flesh at the sight; I drag my tongue through her folds one more time before addressing her. "Hello, little mate."

"Hello, my king." The fingers in my reddish hair pull harder, tearing a few strands out, and I *allow* her to pull me up. Right before doing so, though, I bite her just above her swollen clit—reveling in the way her eyes roll back for a few seconds. Her pretty pink mouth is parted, and her lips are shiny from the lewd way she licked them a second ago.

An act, I don't think she's aware of doing.

"Up." One word, and it's a command from a rightful queen. One I follow until we're chest to chest and her exhale becomes my inhale. Anaya is flushed, skin a healthy glow, and when my eyes dart to the area the poison marred, I find nothing but a faint line the color of blue. "I'm okay."

"Thank the Gods."

"Thank you for protecting me, Leonardo." Lifting a hand, she traces from under my right eye and down my cheek before cupping my chin. "No one has cared for me the way you do. Accepts me as I am."

"You are perfect."

"What I am is yours, Your Highness." A soft smile overtakes her then, this one proudly showing her teeth, and my cock approves, throbbing against her mound and lower abdomen. I'm large and thick with a throbbing head that's leaking pre-come over her skin, rubbing it into her flesh, something she approves of as the tips of her ears and her cheeks blush. As the scent of her arousal thickens, beckoning me to fuck her. "But will you bear my mark? Wear the sign of my imprinting for the rest of your life?"

"Yes."

"And it will be a place of my choosing." Not a question, and I understand. It's part of her nature, one I want to encourage. For her to always be open with me. Faes hold possessions close to their hearts; everything has a meaning or memory attached, and this will be no different.

"Please." My one-word response excites her. Anaya's nostrils flare, and a tiny hand forces my head down to hers for a quick and dominant kiss. And I let her have this moment, giving her what she needs while flipping our positions. I lie beneath her, body at her mercy.

"Oh fuck," she moans, the sound low and throaty while throwing her head back as her wings unfurl. Their shimmery tones are bright again—as if the direct sunlight bathed them—and she stretches each one as if it's a limb. They don't curl around us but rather caress the top of my thighs as she moves slowly down my body.

Anaya takes advantage of my distracted state, and a second later I watch her through hooded eyes as she kisses the head of my dick.

Nuzzles me as more pre-come shoots from the tip, and it glides across her mouth like the most obscene lip oil. "Gods blessed me, Anaya. Fuck, they did."

Her eyes darken as she licks the taste of me from her lips, savoring slowly, and I watch in awe as she gives in to the side of her that's been pushed away for so long. The woman above me is running on instinct—the faes need to mark and fuck, and it makes her ethereal.

"Mine." A low growl, a bit kittenish, and my cock jumps as she wraps a hand around it. Her hold is tight. "You are mine."

"I'm yours."

"Always?"

"Always us. No one else." No sooner has the last word slipped past my lips than she strikes and takes my dick into her warm mouth. She bobs a few times, desperately moaning at my taste, but everything disappears and crashes back into my processors with the force of a battering ram when she sinks her fangs just below the engorged head of my cock. Pain erupts, the sharp sting lasting a second before pleasure crests; I'm taken from one extreme to the other in the same breath, and I come for her.

Rope after rope landing on her tongue and mixing with the blood from the fresh bite that she swallows, yet Anaya lets a little drip over her bottom lip and down to her chin. That, she doesn't lick off. Instead, she mounts me before I can get my breathing under control, poised over me, and tilts her head to the side while wearing a salacious grin.

Dirty and with my come marking her, it's an open invitation.

And in that moment, I understand her.

She took what she needed to feel complete and is now honoring my call for a blood tie to her. Where normally I'd cut our palms and connect us that way, she's giving me a greater gift. Giving me her innocence and life's essence, merging our souls so both the urges and needs of our animal sides are met. Because we're all beholden to our baser instincts.

To hunt. To mate. To procreate.

"I love you, my precious fae. Never forget that." With my hands on her hips, I slam her down on my length in one fast thrust. There's a sharp cry at that, her heated eyes tearing a bit as the final piece of our connection snaps into place. Moreover, if I thought our bond was strong before, this leaves me breathless.

Everything is sharper and more pronounced; from her heart-shaped face and the feel of her cunt wrapped around me, to the way her heartbeat matches mine. How in awe she is of me when I'm the breathless one. Owned.

"Please, Leonardo. Move."

"Not this time, sweetheart. Take your pleasure." Lifting her a few inches off my length, I bring her down again but remain still beneath. I do this a few times and watch pleasure peak in her eyes and the way she bites down on her bottom lip as I hit a particular spot on each stroke. "I want to experience this from your eyes, my mate. Watch you ride me."

"I've never…"

"Neither have I, but we do what feels right. Give your fae what she wants."

That earns me a playful snap of the teeth before she tests a roll of the hips and mewls at the sensation. She does it again, then again, gaining confidence through each gyration until she places both hands on my chest and picks up speed.

The binds that connect us thrash in rapture, from my allowing her the freedom to explore her first time instead of being a forced partici-pant beneath an underserving beast like the man she was promised to. We have our lives ahead of us and plenty of days where I can bend her over and ride her hard, fill her to the brim, and watch her belly bulge from the pressure of my size, but her first time should be special.

And even when every one of my *instincts* demands I take over, I let her control the moment.

"That's it, precious one. You take me so beautifully…the perfect little cunt for her king," I grit out from between clenched teeth when she digs her nails in and breaks the skin of my pecs. An encouragement she likes as the pace of her hips becomes frantic—almost angry with the need to find her release. I can feel it and see it on her face, in the way her mouth forms the perfect *O* with each forceful bounce.

"Leonardo, I'm…Gods…I didn't know," Anaya's words are followed by pressing her chest against mine, leaning fully down on me so I carry her weight. She's getting tired. It's her first time, but that doesn't stop her from bouncing on my dick at a fast pace. Chasing the pleasure that's building inside of me, too.

"Let go." I don't push or thrust, I simply grab an asscheek in each hand and squeeze the round globes. That causes her to clench and my eyes to roll back. It causes pleasurable fire to lick at my every nerve ending before gifting her a sharp slap that tears a hoarse cry from her mouth. "Is that what you need, baby?" I'm given a nod, and that won't do. I smack the other twice. "Words. Use your words."

"Yes." It's nearly a sob, her entire body shuddering atop me, and I give her what she needs. I spank her ass with measured strikes—not too hard or soft—until the writhing woman in my hold comes with a scream. She's clenching and throbbing, trying to pull the come from my balls and once I'm close, I lift her off and bring a breast up to my mouth.

I bite down on the area just above her left nipple as my come spurts from the tip and onto her pussy, marking her with my seed while my teeth break flesh. It's a compulsion—I know it hurts, but I soothe the ache as I slide across her sensitive clit, eliciting a rush of wetness to slip from her tiny hole and kiss the head of my cock.

Her teeth perfectly embedded onto my dick is beautiful, I'm proud of it, but I needed the same. My magic demanded it, and as an apology, I wring another orgasm from her just like this.

Not stopping until her thighs shake and she drops her weight; Anaya's spent body lies on top of me while she tries to calm her breathing. It takes a while for the spasms to wane and her moans to become a little satisfied sigh, but through it all, my female stays where she is while drawing circles on my chest. This is contentment. Bliss. And I slip back inside and lazily pump the rest of my spend into her. I keep a steady rhythm of slow pumps and withdrawals, teasing us as our combined fluids create a heady mess.

It's dripping between her thighs and mine while staining the mattress below; the sweet scent of our blood and come is harmonious and right. Perfection.

Our breathing slows and our bodies relax, but the connection keeps buzzing and I smile at the pretty blonde. I don't say anything to disturb her musings. Talking isn't necessary when our connection is alive and thriving—her emotions are my own—but that doesn't take away from the pride I feel inside my chest when she nips my neck a little while later and says the four words I will never tire of hearing:

I love you, Leonardo.

TEASER

Anaya

OMISSION PART TWO:

I've felt eyes on me all afternoon as the children of the Moore coven show me the spell they learned today. The young ones have been playing out in the fields all morning, learning how to plant blooms—help them grow with a small incantation and the nurturing of each seedling.

They're adorable.

So bright and happy, full of excitement as each performs except a little girl who blushes.

"Are you not ready, Alice?" I ask, keeping my voice soft so as to not draw attention her way. The other children are busy commanding a small grouping of lilies to grow as a gift to me. "You don't have to—"

"Queen Anaya, who's that?" She points to the left of us and toward a giant tree where a man stands. He's leaning against the trunk, casually and unbothered, and every muscle in my body tenses as his smirk widens.

Brice stands without a shirt and his wings are spread, scraping against the forest floor. He's angry at me, the malice in his eyes and aura almost make me cower but I stand my ground. A clear challenge he accepts by crooking a single finger at me before taking off into the sky, and what's worse, he's wearing my father's ring.

The one given to our new king...

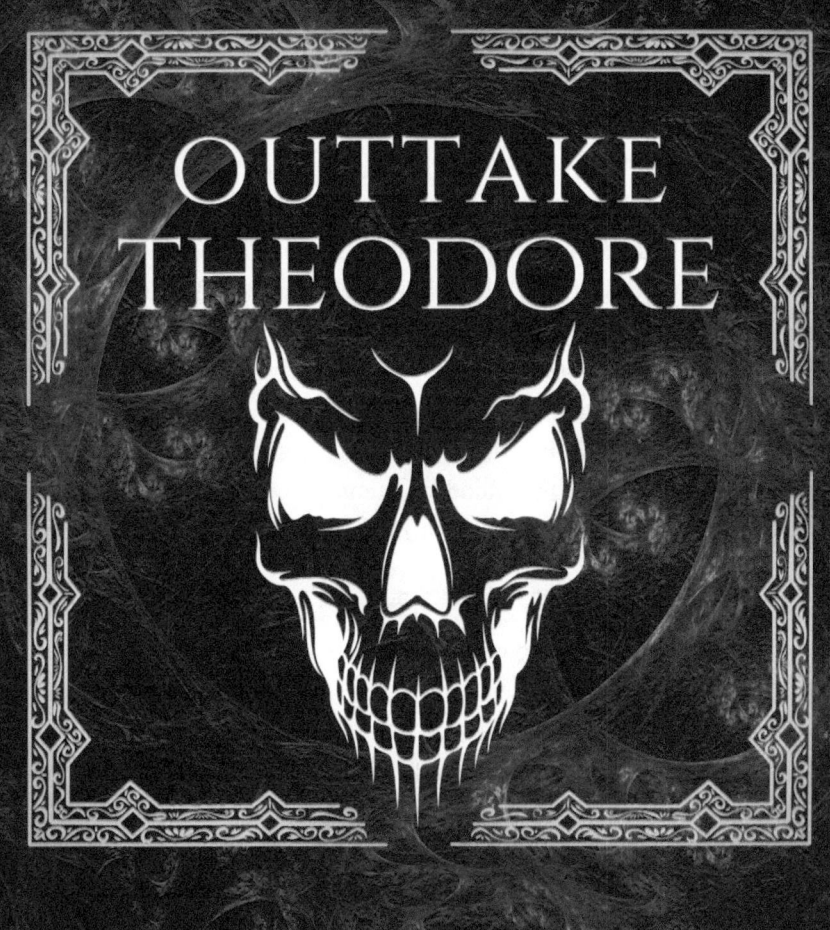

OUTTAKE THEODORE

"Gabriella Astor, what are you doing?" I call out, entering our nursery while my pretty girl stands atop a chair, and places a stack of spell books on the highest shelf. She's six months pregnant, fucking beautiful, and ready to go into labor at any moment. Not that it stops her. If anything, her nesting drives her to move, and clean, and organize everything we touched the day before.

A trait, I admit is utterly crazy yet adorable.

Like I find the way she reaches a hand up, ass bouncing while she gets the grimoire's just right, sinful. But then again, my cock is always hard for her.

My queen. My mate.

"Hey, love." Still not turning to look at me, Gabriella huffs a breath through gritted teeth and then slides them to the opposite corner. She turns them slightly, then changes their stacking order three times, and all the while, I follow each move like the predator I am.

While I've always loved her body, and live for the feel of her pinned beneath me, this is more.

I'm a demon. Born from a god and his desire for a human female—I've fed off the blood of humans for a millennium—and yet, the sight of her swollen with my child brings me down to my knees.

For her. Only ever her.

My beautiful vampiric witch.

She jumps a little when I drag her yoga pants down her lithe thighs, a giggle slipping through when I growl at her. She's not wearing any underwear, completely bare and so wet, and I bite her right asscheek in retaliation.

That ends her amusement, and a second later I'm rewarded with a moan. It's a needy sound. Wanton, but there's something else to it. *Relief?*

My pretty girl's body shivers and goosebumps rise across her sensitive skin, yet it's the drops of wetness that cling to her pussy lips that I'm hypnotized by. I watch them as they slide and gather, and I push her down just a bit with a hand to her lower back, before licking her from clit to clenching hole. Growling against her cunt as her taste explodes on my tongue, my eyes rolling back while beads of pre-come slip from my engorged head.

Yet I ignore it. My need.

This is about her. Gabriella's been tense and worried and she's so fucking beautiful—it is my privilege to worship her. Because I live for her pleasure-fueled noises. Those little kittenish mewls that come from the back of her throat, and I'm rewarded with one when I slide a finger into her pussy.

"Oh fuck, my king," she purrs, opening her thighs as much as the chair allows. "That feels so good."

"Naughty girl. You knew, didn't you?" That earns her a sharp spank to the ass that I soothe a second later with a kiss. I'm sliding three thick fingers inside, testing her dilation and my pretty girl is close. *Why didn't she tell me?* "How long have you been in labor?"

"Since this morning," she grits out, pushing back against my hand, but then groans when I pull out. Through our bond, I can feel how much she needs this. The release to help ease her aches—as the rest of her body becomes tense—riddled with the pains of a contraction. "Please, Theo. I need—"

"I'll always give you what you need, pretty girl. I got you." Standing, I pick her up by the waist and walk us into the adjacent birthing room. From conception, we chose to make this a private moment between the two of us—no healers or midwife—we'd tend to our child and announce the birth a week after.

We equipped the space with a large round bed and dimmed lighting, while a large humidifier spread a replica of my scent throughout the room. It helps to calm her; a thoughtful gift from Isabella after learning about our pregnancy.

"Fuck, this hurts." She whimpers as I strip her down and place her in the center of the mattress. I'm quick to undress, placing my body behind hers before pulling Gabriella into my chest. Let her lean on me. "I can feel the baby moving down. The pressure—"

"Breathe with me, love. Let your body do what it needs to." With firm strokes, I begin massaging down her arm and then her fingers before slowly rubbing soothing circles across her swollen stomach. And it's then I feel the ripple of a contraction, how every muscle in her body locks down tight before a pain-filled cry slips from her mouth. "It will be over soon, pretty girl. You're doing so good."

"I should've told you earlier," Gabby pants, falling forward and onto all fours. She's gripping the bedding, her blood-red eyes looking back at me. "A magazine online said sex helps move things along, and I made it worse."

"Nothing you do is ever wrong." That earns me a watery grin. The tears will never fall, but I feel the same way. We've wanted this for so long. "Our little one's just excited and ready to meet its kingdom. He or she will be the perfect mini dictator."

"I love you, Theodore Astor. With everything I am."

"As do I, my queen. In every life." A vow that she follows with a guttural scream. Her fangs drop and pierce her bottom lip while her eyes remain on mine, never wavering as she pushes. Her nails shred the bedsheets, tearing easily through the mattress, and I'm caging her body until the head crowns.

On her next whimper, I have her turned around and facing me while my fangs break the skin of her neck. It settles her instantaneously, yet I don't retract them. We stay this way through each contraction, connected and celebrating our love while she sighs into my bite.

"It's time, my king." There's a drowsy quality to her tone now, and I feel through our link as she melts into the pain. Gabriella welcomes the next contraction with a smile on her face and I release her, placing both hands between her thighs and watch in awe as our baby girl is born.

And as her little mouth crinkles and opens, an enormous yawn escaping her, my world changes for the second time.

The love I have for my daughter knows no bounds or measures. This is pure and all-consuming, and I'm humbled by the gift given to us by the gods.

"Welcome to the world, Beloved Rose Astor."

"Beloved?" my pretty girl asks, eyes shining and smile a bit watery, as I guide her with one hand toward the mountain of pillows we never used. She lets me adjust her without complaint, though— and the split second while I hold them both—causes my once cold heart to thump harshly inside my chest. "Gods, she's perfect."

"Just like her mother." Placing her atop Gabriella's chest, I lean down and kiss both my girls before checking my mate over. She's still bleeding a bit, but the vampiric side of her is aiding in her healing. "She's mostly you with a touch of me, and nothing is more precious than that. Our Beloved Rose Astor."

"I wonder what we'll name our future son, then? We have to give him something just as meaningful."

At her comment, my head snaps in her direction. A smirk tugs at my lips. "You want more children, pretty girl?"

"I do." Gabby's counting Beloved's tiny fingers and then her toes, completely enamored. "I want an entire vampire coven with you, my king."

Turn the page for Omission news...

COVER COMING SOON

DUET PART 2

OMISSION

FATE'S BITE SERIES

ELENA M REYES

Hi, my loves!!!

After much deliberation and going back and forth over the plot of this entire series, I've decided to make OMISSION a duet! There's so much story to tell—so much happening—and I don't want to leave anything out.

I want to make you feel and scream and cheer for this couple.

I want to give you all the growly warlock king taking his precious mate over—the edge of his desk, a couch, or tree trunk—with one finger in her ass while riding her hard, moments. Or maybe they'll play a game of hide-and-fuck.

(The number of people who get the: touch her and die in this duet is… ;)

I couldn't do that in just 1 book. Not without shortchanging, you, the reader, and I refuse to do that. I appreciate you guys too much, and I'm so thankful for all the love and support you have given me this year while I deal with health issues. So keep an eye out; I'll have more information coming soon.

The cover designer is booked, and I can't wait to see what she does with this one. The second part of this DUET will be published in early March 2024!!!!

I love you so much!
Elena XoXo

PRE-ORDER HERE:
https://books2read.com/Omission-Book-2

FATE'S BITE SERIES

LITTLE LIES
LITTLE MATE
HALF TRUTHS DUET
HALF TRUTHS: THEN
HALF TRUTHS: NOW
OMISSION DUET
OMISSION (Part One)
OMISSION (Part Two)
TERO (TBD)
MARCIA (TBD)

ABOUT THE AUTHOR

Elena M. Reyes was born and raised in Miami, Florida. She is the epitome of a Floridian and if she could live in her beloved flip-flops, she would.

As a small child, she was always intrigued with all forms of art—whether it was dancing to island rhythms, or painting with any medium she could get her hands on. Her first taste of writing came to her during her fifth-grade year when her class was prompted to participate in the D. A. R. E. Program and write an essay on what they'd learned.

Her passion for reading over the years has amassed her with hours of pleasure. It wasn't until she stumbled upon fanfiction that her thirst to write overtook her world. She now resides in Central Florida with her husband and son, spending all her down time letting her creativity flow and characters grow.

Website: https://www.elenamreyes.com/

Find My Books Here:
https://www.bookbub.com/authors/elena-m-reyes

Email: Reyes139ff@gmail.com

facebook.com/ElenaMReyesAuthor
x.com/ElenaMReyes
instagram.com/elenar139
tiktok.com/@authorelenamreyes
bookbub.com/profile/elena-m-reyes

ALSO BY ELENA M. REYES

FATE'S BITE SERIES

LITTLE LIES

LITTLE MATE

HALF TRUTHS: THEN

HALF TRUTHS: NOW

OMISSION (PART ONE)

OMISSION (PART TWO)

TERO (TBD)

MARCIA (TBD)

BEAUTIFUL SINNER SERIES

Each book is a standalone.

Now Live!

SIN (#1)

COVET (#2)

MINE (#3)

YOURS (#4)

RISQUE #5

OWN #6

Beautiful Sinner Spin-Off

CORRUPT

MY SINFUL VALENTINE

SAVAGE KISS

ONE RULE
(BOOK #2 LIONEL TBD)

(Marked Series)
Marking Her #1
Marking Him #2
Scars #2.5
Marked #3

(I Saw You)
I Saw You
I Love You #1.5

Teasing Hands Duet
Teasing Hands #1
Taunting Lips #2

SAFE ROMANCE:
Taste Of You
Doctor's Orders
Back To You

STANDALONES:
Craving Sugar
Stolen Kisses